I0740953

Also by Marian D. Schwartz

Realities

The Writers' Conference

Harry Danced Divinely: Collected Giffort Street Stories

War on Giffort Street, a novella

Sara Barefield

THE LAST SEASON
THE STORY OF A MARRIAGE

MARIAN D. SCHWARTZ

III

The Last Season, The Story of a Marriage is a work of fiction. The characters and events portrayed in this book are the product of the author's imagination. Any resemblance to actual persons, living or dead, events, or places is entirely coincidental and not intended by the author.

The Last Season, The Story of a Marriage

Marian D. Schwartz

ISBN 978-0-9886076-2-0

Gristmill Publishing, L.L.C.

To Paul

"Now there's three things you can do in a baseball game. You can win, you can lose, or it can rain."

- Casey Stengel

"Yessuh, baseball is more than a little bit like life."

- Red Barber

MARIAN D. SCHWARTZ

Prologue

The field was in a sad state, the grass burned to a scruffy brown and the paths between the bases worn to hard gray dirt. The men on the field, all middle-aged and showing various signs of wear, were oblivious to the condition of the field, the heavy evening heat, and the fiery glare of the setting sun. It was the bottom of the ninth inning. The home team was up: there were two outs; the bases were loaded. The score was 9-8 in favor of the visitors. The batter, a stocky man whose cap was pulled so low on his forehead that it was a wonder he could see at all, stood hunched over the plate as if the burden of a full count were weighing him down. He watched the ball leave the pitcher's hand with every bit of concentration he possessed, the muscles in his aging body tense, and when he felt the bat connect solidly with the ball and heard that glorious CRACK, he felt better than he'd ever felt in his life.

It was a line drive. The third baseman leaped toward the bag, extending the full length of his body until he was, impossibly, nearly parallel with the ground. It was a leap that defied gravity, a leap accomplished with the grace of a ballet dancer, the motion so fluid and clean that it was breathtaking. There was a loud THWACK as he snared the ball in the pocket of his glove.

His descent wasn't nearly as graceful, but Buddy Middleton would have laughed at the idea of comparing his athlete's grace to a ballet dancer's. At that moment he had the ball snug in the pocket of his glove. He could still make a decent catch at fifty. Buddy was a happy, happy man.

Ginger

I

It all started the night of the Thackers' party. The party, a housewarming, was called for seven thirty. At eight thirty Buddy still wasn't home. He'd warned me he might be a little late, but an hour was more than just a little. I kept going to the living room window and looking out, as if somehow my presence there would draw him home. My stomach was churning with either hunger or aggravation, or both. During one of my trips to the window it occurred to me that I had spent over half my life waiting for Buddy to finish playing ball, and I still got upset when he was late, which was often. It also occurred to me that I was the only one who seemed to mind. Buddy played ball so well—baseball, racquetball, tennis, golf—that people were willing to forgive him anything. When I occasionally complained, they looked at me as though I were a bad sport.

His car pulled into the driveway at eight thirty-five. He came into the house through the door to the garage and called, "Ginger."

"In the living room," I said as evenly as I could. I took a deep breath and let it out slowly, trying to expel my irritation. It was a trick I had learned early in our marriage when I realized that holding on to my anger wouldn't make Buddy come home on time. There was no point in spoiling the evening.

He came up the steps from the foyer to the living room with his hands raised, palms open in a gesture of peace. He looked like an aging kid, a sweaty, dirty fifty-year-old man wearing a T-shirt, shorts, and a beat-up baseball cap. "I'm sorry," he said. Then he gazed at me a moment. "Wow," he said, the expression on his face anything but juvenile.

I backed away as he stepped closer. "The party's called for seven thirty."

His eyes gleamed suggestively. "You look terrific, and we're already late anyway. Maybe I can tempt you when I get out of the shower."

"No way," I said. "A shirt and slacks are on the bed."

Before he went upstairs, he turned. "You really do look great."

I had tried especially hard to look well that evening. Jane Thacker is my best friend, and I had helped her plan the party. Although the only thing I bought was a turquoise silk blouse to go with a pair of white slacks I already owned, it was important to me that I look my best. I had had my hair re-frosted to hide the gray the week before, and I had taken special care with my make-up. Buddy detests make-up, so I use it as subtly as possible. But as I've explained to him more times than I'd care to count, there isn't a woman over thirty whose appearance can't be improved with make-up. And when a woman reaches my age—forty-eight—she needs all the help she can get. That evening, the turquoise blouse made the difference. Turquoise is my best color; it brings out my eyes, which are a gray-blue, and it's a perfect complement to blond-streaked hair and a light tan. Whenever I want to look especially well, I wear turquoise.

Buddy was back in twenty minutes, wearing the shirt and slacks I had put out for him. I had the clothes ready to save time. Buddy doesn't care much about clothes, though he looks well in them. He's just a shade under six feet tall and still nicely built; since his life is centered on sports, he keeps himself in shape. He has a spectacular butt, which women notice. His hair was brown but is now quite gray; however, he still looks boyish because his face is full, as is his grin. Buddy's smile is wonderful, full of energy and life.

I put down the book I was reading. "Let's go," I said.

"Where's Zack?"

"At the movies with Nancy."

He started to open the door, then paused. He smelled fresh and clean. "I don't suppose I could convince you to skip the party and head upstairs."

"You're impossible!" I said, though if it had been someone else's party I would have been tempted.

Buddy grinned. Laugh lines spread from the corners of his eyes. "You can't blame a guy for trying."

The Thackers live in a subdivision called Saddleford, though there isn't a horse to saddle or a river to ford anywhere near it. Saddleford is the nicest subdivision in the county. The lots are all two acres or more, and the houses are restricted to a minimum of three thousand square feet. I sold the Thackers their land. I was in real estate when Saddleford opened, and I knew it would be a smart investment. The developer was Avery Laird, so they couldn't miss. Laird has made millions in real estate; people call him "the man with the Midas touch."

The Thackers' house is enormous: three bedrooms, each with a private bath, a master suite with a sitting room and the largest, most sumptuous bathroom I've ever seen, a sunroom, a den, and of course the requisite living room, dining room, family room, kitchen, powder room, and laundry room. Only Jane and Cal live in the house; their daughters, both in their twenties, are grown and gone.

We were late arriving at the party, so we had to park a considerable distance from the house. "It looks like they invited everyone they know," Buddy commented after we had walked for several minutes passing expensive cars parked bumper-to-bumper.

There was an edge in his voice that I tried to ignore. Although Buddy is fond of Jane, over the years he has developed a real dislike for Cal. Jane and Cal used to live a few doors away from us; we were in our twenties then, and our children were babies. Cal owned a furniture store and was struggling to make a living. Buddy was doing the same thing he's doing now: teaching and coaching. Eventually Cal switched from furniture to appliances. In a desperate effort to raise money, he gave deep discounts on the appliances, and his business took off. Today Cal

Thacker is the discount appliance king of Central New York State. The name Cal is synonymous with refrigerators and washing machines. I don't know why, but for some reason Cal has always insisted upon letting Buddy know how well he's doing. It's as if he's keeping score: his financial success versus Buddy's successes as an athlete and coach. Maybe Cal's trying to compensate for his physical awkwardness; he's a big man—six two or three and heavily built—and a real klutz. He admires Buddy and would like to be his friend, but everything he says seems to end up being alienating. Maybe he's been selling so long that he doesn't know when to stop. When the Thackers moved into a bigger, nicer house, Buddy commented that the neighborhood had improved. As we walked up the circular driveway to this newest, latest Thacker house, sleek and contemporary, I didn't want to think about how Buddy would react. I reached for his hand. "Let's have a good time," I said.

"We will," he said, "after the party."

Jane was the first to greet us as we walked through the double-door entrance. She looked chic in a silk blouse and slacks that were a luscious raspberry. Her jewelry was impressive but also in good taste; she was wearing diamond stud earrings at least a carat each, a thick gold omega necklace that had a simple diamond slide, and a heavy gold wedding band set with one enormous diamond. Her brown hair was pulled back and tied with a raspberry ribbon.

Jane isn't a pretty woman. She has a long, narrow face and dark, sallow skin, but she's one of the finest people I've ever known, considerate and caring, a loyal and good friend. She smiled warmly. Her teeth are her best feature, perfectly even and very white. "That must have been some game. I had almost given up on you two," she said, kissing me and then Buddy. "You have to be starving. Do you want drinks first or would you prefer to head straight for the food?"

"I want it all!" Buddy said with a grin.

Jane laughed. "Give me your drink orders and I'll head for the bar while you help yourselves in the dining room."

We were about to step into the dining room when Cal spotted us. "The Middletons," he boomed, announcing our presence—or perhaps our tardiness— to everyone within earshot.

He strode across the polished marble foyer floor carrying an empty plate. "Ginger, great to see you," he said, bending to kiss me.

I averted my face so his wet kiss would land on my cheek. He smelled of booze and garlic. My stomach rumbled.

Either Cal didn't hear my stomach or he chose to ignore it. He shook Buddy's hand vigorously. "How was your game?" he said. Without waiting for a reply, he continued, "You haven't seen the house yet, have you? Come with me. I'll give you the deluxe tour. Wait'll you see the master bath. It's big enough to hold a convention in, and you can swim in the Jacuzzi."

Fortunately, Jane returned with our drinks. "Why aren't you in the dining room?" she said.

Cal shot her a look of irritation. "I was just about to give them the grand tour."

"They haven't eaten," she said, her gaze resting

briefly on the empty plate in Cal's hand.

"Oh," he said. "I'll wait while you fill your plates and then we'll go."

"They might want to sit at one of the tables on the deck or the lawn and relax while they eat. It's so pleasant there. We've had such great luck tonight with the weather. Why don't you catch up with Buddy later. Ginger's seen the house so many times she must be sick of it."

Cal wasn't happy, but he accepted her suggestion. Even now as I remember it I am amazed at how sweetly she spoke to him, without any impatience or annoyance at his lack of manners. If Buddy had been that insensitive to guests in our home, I'd have talked to him through clenched teeth.

The dining room table was picked over, but there was still plenty to eat. Jane, always fearful that there won't be enough, must have told the caterer to prepare for twice the number of people invited. There was sliced beef tenderloin, turkey, rolls, relishes, a variety of pasta salads, cheeses, and fresh cut-up fruit and vegetables. Desserts and coffee were on the buffet. I knew there had been shrimp, but it was gone. Shrimp never lasts long. People always seem to forget their manners and gorge themselves on it.

Ellie and Neil Hamilton were sitting at the only table on the deck that had room for us. There were empty places at tables on the lawn, but if we had gone further it would have been rude. Ellie and Neil are nice people. Although we were never close friends, we enjoyed seeing them until their son, Jason, died tragically. Jason went to a rock concert with a group of boys that included our son, Zack. The seats at the concert weren't assigned, and in the rush to get in, Jason was trampled to death. It happened five years ago. Jason and Zack were the same age.

For a long time the cloud of Jason's death hung over our family, especially Buddy. Late at night he would check on Zack the way he did when the boys were infants; he'd open Zack's bedroom door and stand in the darkness, listening to him breathe. There were nights when Buddy woke Zack, who is a light sleeper. Zack never complained. Instead, he went out of his way to tell us his plans, where he was going and what he'd be doing and what time he thought he'd be home. Zack had his own recovery to make over Jason's death, yet he helped and comforted us as well. Together we all felt the fragility of life.

As I said, Ellie and Neil are nice people, but whenever we see them we are reminded of Jason. We are reminded that through a cruel twist of fate our son is alive and their son is dead. Buddy says they've asked about Zack since the time the boys were in Little League together. Perhaps that is so, but I wasn't conscious of it until Jason died.

There were two other couples at the table besides the Hamiltons: Rosemary and Douglas Tanner, whom we knew, and a man and a woman who appeared to be in their mid-thirties. Rosemary Tanner, a freckled redhead who is Buddy's age, introduced us to the couple. "This is Hilary and Cordell Wylie," she said. "Cordell is the owner and editor of *Forum* magazine."

Cordell stood up and extended his hand. He's approximately my height, five feet seven, and slightly built. His hair is sandy brown and he wears it long, curling over his shirt collar. "Pleased to meet you," he drawled.

"A Southerner," I said, surprised. "Where are you from?"

"Chapel Hill, North Carolina. It takes me until July to thaw out from your winters."

We started talking about the past winter, which had a couple of really brutal storms, and about the well-kept secret that our annual snowfall is higher than Buffalo's. Somehow the conversation turned to sports, which inevitably happens when Buddy is around. Cordell expressed an interest in having someone on his staff do an article on Buddy for *Forum*. "You're a local celebrity," he said. "People would enjoy reading about you."

"They've heard so much about me over the years, they're tired of me," Buddy said. "What you need for that slick magazine of yours is an interview with someone mysterious yet well-known, a person who goes out of his way to avoid the limelight. Someone like Avery Laird. An interview with him would sell copies."

"Don't I know it!" Cordell said. "But he's impossible. He absolutely refuses to be interviewed, and his staff sees to it that no one he doesn't want to talk to can get through to him."

"Eventually someone will get an interview with him," Neil Hamilton said.

"How?" Cordell said.

Neil gave a slight smile. He's an attorney; he has a reputation for being a sharp negotiator, particularly in divorces. "The way these things usually happen. An enterprising person will have something he wants."

"I appreciate what you're saying, but I know how

hard people have tried to get to Laird. From where I'm sitting, I don't think it can be done."

Neil shrugged. He looked unconvinced.

The Wylies left the table soon after that, as did the Tanners. "Neil," I said, "do you really think it's possible to get to Avery Laird?"

"Sure. You just have to find the right key to open the lock."

"That sounds reasonable," I said, "but Laird owns all the keys."

Neil's angular features sharpened. For the briefest moment he reminded me of an eagle or a hawk, so sharp-sighted that nothing escaped him. "No one owns all the keys. At one time or another everyone wants something. It takes work, as well as patience and perseverance, to figure out what that something is."

Wanting to change the subject, I asked Ellie what she thought of the Thackers' house. Ellie is a petite blond whose features are as soft as her husband's are sharp. "It's gorgeous," she said. "I've never seen anything like that master bathroom, all marble and mirrors. It looks like it was plucked out of a magazine."

We talked about houses, and then about empty nests. The Hamiltons asked about Steve and Zack, and we asked about their daughter, who is several years younger than Zack. It was easier to talk about Zack than it had been in the past, but I still thought of Jason and felt Ellie and Neil's sorrow.

Buddy and I circulated for the rest of the evening, drifting in different directions as we usually do. I made a point of speaking to Cordell Wylie before the evening was over. "Do you ever accept unsolicited articles for *Forum*?" I asked.

"Occasionally," he said. "Are you a writer?"

There was a subtle change in his expression. His face was less open, his eyes more guarded. I suddenly realized that he was probably approached by aspiring writers all the time and saw myself as he must have been seeing me—a middle-aged woman dreaming of a new career. "I was a journalism major in college," I said. "I'm inquiring because of your comments about Avery Laird. If I did manage to get an interview with him, would you consider publishing it?"

"Sure," he said so off-handedly that I knew he was positive it would never happen.

"How many words would you want?"

"Three thousand or so."

I thanked him and then moved on, determined to get the interview if for no other reason than to prove to him that I could get it and do a creditable job.

It was after midnight when Buddy and I left the party. On our way home I asked him what he thought of the Thackers' new house. "It's the best that money can buy," he said.

"That was mean."

"Maybe," he conceded, "but it's also true. The house is too big for just the two of them. What do they need all those bedrooms and bathrooms for?"

"Jane wants to have plenty of room when the girls come home with their husbands and children."

Buddy chuckled. "Neither one of them is married yet."

I knew what he was thinking: the Thacker girls aren't particularly attractive. "Well," I said, "Jane's ready."

He reached for my hand across the car seat. "You know I'd give you a retirement palace if I could."

"I know," I sighed, "I know."

Buddy knew what I was thinking. We've been married for so long—twenty-seven years—we can communicate with a sigh, with a gesture so small that it's barely noticeable. He was not going to allow me to feel sorry for myself or for us because we couldn't afford a luxurious new home on his salary. "You, however, could have given us a jazzy house if you'd stayed in real estate. I could have showed off the fruits of your labors: *look at what my wife is providing for us.* I could have even quit coaching and learned how to cook. I could have had delicious dinners waiting for you every night. Can you imagine..."

"Enough, Buddy," I said, laughing.

Neither one of us acknowledged how much we had both hated my career in real estate, nor that I had quit because the market had skidded downhill.

Zack was still out when we got home. After we went upstairs to our bedroom, I recalled something I'd heard at the party. "I understand you made a phenomenal catch tonight."

"Yeah," he said, reaching for me, "and now I'm going to make an even better one."

We undressed quickly, as hungry for each other as we had been when we were first married.

II

I didn't think about Avery Laird and the article for *Forum* until the beginning of September. Our son Steve came home a week after the Thackers' party and stayed until the end of August, a short but full visit of six days.

Steve spent the summer working for a Wall Street law firm. He was paid an unbelievable amount of money, a good portion of which he was able to save because he stayed at a friend's apartment. He'll need every cent of it. His last year at Harvard Law School will cost more than Buddy makes in a year, well over sixty thousand dollars, providing he doesn't incur any unusual expenses. He'll supplement his financial aid package with his savings from the summer and a part-time job; we'll cover the rest.

Of our two sons, Steve is the one who inherited our best genes: Buddy's athletic ability and my father's looks. My father was an exceptionally handsome man; he had strong, clean features and good coloring. Steve's eyes are replicas of his, a clear blue surrounded by thick lashes. Buddy claims Steve's brains as well; he says they come from his father. I believe they come from my side of the family.

Everything always came easily to Steve: sports, grades, girls. Whatever he wanted, he got. He was the starting quarterback for three out of four years in high school and set records that still haven't been broken. His name and picture were on the sports pages so often that I felt as though we were living with a celebrity. With a population of approximately one hundred thousand people, Clinton Falls still has a small town interest in its athletes.

I was never comfortable with Steve playing football. It is a brutal sport. Boys have had their necks broken on football fields; some have been permanently paralyzed; some have died. When I told Buddy about a university course on violence that made attendance at football games mandatory, he laughed. "Football is more American than apple pie," he said.

Buddy always tried to whisk away my fears of Steve getting injured by pointing out that the quarterback is the most protected player on the team. He didn't seem to be concerned. Maybe he thought Steve would escape any serious injuries because his reflexes are so quick. Maybe he thought Steve would be lucky because he'd always been lucky, a golden boy who would have a golden career throwing touchdown passes. Even in the beginning, when Steve first started playing football, Buddy wasn't worried. "Why don't you steer him into baseball instead?" I asked.

"Steve has to make his own choices," Buddy said.

After being courted by colleges for more than two years, Steve decided to go to the University of Michigan. I was glad to finally see the end of all the calls and the visits; there were times when it felt like college reps were taking over our lives. It was quite an education. I learned the various codes the different colleges use to make sure the athletes they want are accepted. Steve was instructed to put specific symbols—usually X's or C's—in the upper corners on certain pages of his applications. Depending upon the college, either points were added to his SATs to ensure his acceptance or his application was pushed right through. There isn't a college in this country, from the loftiest Ivy League school to the smallest state university, that doesn't make exceptions for the athletes it wants. When Zack was filling out his college applications, I was tempted to tell him the codes. I wanted him to have the easy ride that his brother did, not that Zack needed charity. He's a decent basketball player and an honor student; he just wasn't the star that Steve was.

As happy as I was to see the last of the college reps that courted Steve, I sensed that Buddy missed them. He'd loved to sit and talk sports with all those college people. It was as if he were being courted as well. And he was probably thinking of his own glory days and how much better it would be for his son.

In the final few seconds of the last quarter in a game against Ohio State in Steve's junior year at Michigan, he was caught off balance by a linebacker as he let go of a pass. Steve went down hard, the linebacker on top of him. Buddy and I were in the stands. We saw the linebacker get up and Steve remain on the ground. Over one hundred thousand people were roaring. Steve's pass had been completed for Michigan's winning touchdown.

The bones in Steve's wrist were shattered; the tendon to his thumb was torn. Fortunately, the game was in Ann Arbor. The University of Michigan has huge medical complex, buildings that go on for miles. Steve was in the operating room for what seemed like ten lifetimes. When the doctor came out afterward, he told us he didn't know how successful the surgery would be, that Steve would never be able to play football again.

I couldn't look at Buddy. I experienced a rush of relief so strong that it felt like knots of worry I had carried for years had suddenly dissolved. Although I am not a religious person, I closed my eyes and thanked God that Steve would be all right and that he would never play football again.

Steve worked harder regaining the use of his hand than he had ever worked in his life. Instead of receiving the instant gratification he'd always gotten from sports, he had to do hours of exercises to achieve the major victory of gripping his toothbrush. In some respects his injury was one of the best things that had ever happened to him. For the first time he learned what it meant to work and struggle without getting immediate results. He learned the meaning of patience.

Zack wouldn't let Steve quit. He called Steve at school several times a week to find out how his therapy was going, and he worked with him at home during winter break. He developed an uncanny ability to sense when Steve was faltering and always managed to keep him on track. Today Steve tells everyone that if it weren't for his brother's support and encouragement, he wouldn't have gotten his hand back.

Before Steve was injured I had been concerned that he was becoming arrogant. I'd begun noticing acts of thoughtlessness and a lack of consideration for Zack and Buddy and me. Steve had become very focused on himself and his POTENTIAL, spelled in capital letters. PROFESSIONAL FOOTBALL. FAME. BIG MONEY. Not only did his injury force him to make many adjustments, but he learned to appreciate acts of kindness that he would have been oblivious to in the past. Though in some respects it was a tragedy for him and for Buddy, I see it as a lucky break, no pun intended.

Buddy and I have never really talked about Steve's injury. I know how deeply disappointed he was when the doctor told us about Steve's wrist. Buddy had a chance at a career in professional baseball but walked away from it. There are tears in the fabric of a marriage that can't be mended, and that is a tear which was always in ours. Buddy had looked forward to Steve's career in football; it would have given him a taste of what he had missed. I felt bad for him, but I was afraid to say anything. Buddy never mentions it; neither do I.

Zack cut his hours at the pool where he worked as a lifeguard so he could spend time with Steve during the six days Steve was home. He had been quieter than usual all summer, as if he were preoccupied with something. At first Buddy thought the cause might be Nancy Spaulding, a girl Zack had been seeing on-and-off for nearly a year. "He's finally been hooked," Buddy said.

I disagreed. Zack's attitude toward Nancy was

too casual to cause the change in his behavior. "He likes her, but he isn't in love with her," I said.

"How do you know?"

"If he doesn't talk to her for two or three days, it doesn't bother him."

Buddy couldn't argue with that.

The first few days Steve was home he and Zack did a lot of talking. Although I couldn't hear what they were saying, the low buzz of their voices drifted through the house; it was a nice sound, pleasant and companionable. To see them so close was a reward for the years when they had squabbled. I wondered what they were talking about, but I didn't have to wonder long. At dinner the second night of Steve's visit, Zack told us that he'd decided to apply to medical school.

Buddy and I looked at him, dumbfounded. In less than a week he was due back at school for his last year in engineering. Finally, Buddy said, "What about engineering?"

Zack shrugged. His shoulders are narrower than Buddy's and Steve's; he's tall and lanky. He has Buddy's neat nose and full grin, but the grin doesn't come as easily to him as it does to Buddy. "I'll get my degree in engineering," he said. "I just won't use it."

"Don't you have to take specific courses and some kind of admission test to go to medical school?" I asked.

"I have the math and all the science," he said, "and I took the MCAT in the spring."

"He scored in the eighty-ninth percentile," Steve said proudly.

"Sounds good," Buddy said.

"It's better than good!" Steve said. "It's great!

He'll have no trouble getting in, and I'll be earning enough to help financially. I should be starting at one hundred thousand a year or better, so I'll be able to make a hefty contribution."

Buddy and I looked at each other. His eyes shone with pride; mine were brimming with tears of happiness. We were both thinking the same thing: that we'd raised fine boys. He winked at me and I smiled. We'd had many good times in our marriage, but I can't recall a better moment than that one.

Later Zack explained that he'd been unhappy in engineering for a while. A flash of hurt crossed Buddy's face. He'd always wanted the boys to feel that they could come to us to discuss whatever was on their minds. "When did this unhappiness begin?" he asked, sounding as if he felt betrayed.

"It started toward the end of the second semester of my sophomore year. The courses I was taking were hard, and what made them even harder was that they were boring. I just wasn't interested. I thought it would get better in my junior year, but after the first few weeks I knew it wouldn't. I felt like I had made a wrong turn and couldn't get my bearings."

"Why didn't you say something?" Buddy said.

"Because you would have worried about it, which wouldn't have helped," Zack said. "I needed to look around. I knew what I didn't want to be—a teacher, a businessman, a lawyer—so I figured I would stay where I was until I found what I wanted. Then I met a guy who had cancer and was fitted with an artificial arm. I was fascinated with what the arm could do. Suddenly something clicked: the arm, engineering, medicine. Even Steve's wrist. It all came together."

At that moment it came together for me, too. Zack hadn't told us because he knew we couldn't afford medical school unless I went back to work. He had disliked my career in real estate as much as I did. So Zack went to Steve, not for money I'm sure, but for advice. And Steve showed him how to do it: he'd go to a state school, take out loans, and Steve and Buddy and I would cover as much as we could.

Money. The remainder of the evening I thought about money. I thought about Zack's hesitation to tell us what he wanted to do with his life because we didn't have enough money. He'd spent the entire summer at home and hadn't uttered a word. I went to bed with my head spinning.

Ironically, it was Zack who nudged me into real estate again by inadvertently uncovering the path to Avery Laird. The day before he left for school he asked me if I had any plans for the fall. We were in the kitchen eating lunch. He knew I'd been restless and bored. I told him about my conversation with Cordell Wylie. "I really want to do that interview with Avery Laird," I said, "but I can't think of a way to get to him."

"There was an article about Laird in the paper last month when you and Dad were at the cottage. He's bought all the land on a block between Main and Seneca Streets to build a mall except for one property, which some woman won't sell. He owns the entire parcel except for her piece."

Zack shook his head and smiled. "The article was mostly about her. She's a tough old lady. Laird refused to comment. Actually, the real news was that he owns all that land. He set up a dummy corporation to buy it."

"Thanks," I said, jumping up to give him a hug.

"What did I do?"

"I think you've just given me my ticket to Avery Laird."

III

I waited until Zack left for school before embarking on my plan to get the interview. There were some hard moments for me when his car pulled out of the driveway. I couldn't lose the feeling that he wouldn't be back for a full summer again. I never experienced that feeling with Steve, perhaps because I know we still had a few years left with Zack, or maybe because I'm not as close to Steve. When he was growing up, sports were Steve's world. If he wasn't out playing ball, he was buried in the sports section of the newspaper or reading a book or magazine about sports. Zack played ball, too, but he wasn't consumed by sports. I could talk to him about almost anything. And during the football and baseball seasons, when Buddy's coaching duties kept him away from home and made him tense when he was around (which hasn't changed), Zack's company was a joy. He has a way of listening, of tilting his head to one side and looking at you as if there is nothing more important in the world than what you are saying. Zack has listened this way from the time he was a toddler. I think I'll miss that the most.

It was a magnificent morning when I set out for

the *Clinton Falls Gazette*, one of those perfect days in early September in which there is a suggestion of fall in the late summer air. Maybe it was the weather, but for the first time in ages I had a feeling of anticipation, as though anything were possible.

I knew when the article about Avery Laird and the property he wanted was published, so it wasn't difficult to get a copy. Buddy and I had spent the last weekend in July at my parents' cottage. The cottage is on the shore of Lake Ontario, which is about an hour's drive from Clinton Falls. Every summer of my childhood was spent there. After the boys were born, my father had an addition built so there would be enough room for all of us: my parents, Buddy and me, and the boys. My mother considered selling the cottage after my father died six years ago, but I persuaded her to keep it. Despite the polluted water and encroaching development, I couldn't imagine a summer passing without going there. Now it is rented except for a week that my mother reserves for us. Usually we spend just a few days, which Buddy says is enough.

Buddy wanted my mother to sell the cottage. He doesn't particularly enjoy it and only goes there because it is important to me. He thinks my attachment to it is somehow linked to the fact that I'm an only child. I don't see the connection, but whatever the case, the cottage is a part of my life, a touchstone that marks the rhythm of the seasons, the passing of years. Even before we turn into the long gravel driveway my head starts filling with memories.

The article on Avery Laird was in the paper on the Saturday we were gone. Luckily, there was also a picture of the woman, Geneva Stratton, standing in front of her property—a two-story brick building, the lower half of which had a boarded-up store front. Above the store there was a sad-looking sign that said *Stratton's Variety Store*. The number 1801 was clearly visible above the front door.

I was familiar with Stratton's Variety Store, as well as the block that Avery Laird wanted to develop. It's toward the lower end of Main Street, which was a thriving area until the first suburban mall was built in Clinton Falls. The mall, developed by Avery Laird, hurt a large number of downtown retail businesses. That particular block was one of the first to falter; some businesses moved to follow the population while others simply lingered, stretching out their days with outdated stock and dusty shelves.

While I was at the *Clinton Falls Gazette*, I looked up the woman's telephone number. There was no listing for Geneva Stratton in the phone book; nor was there a Stratton listed on Main Street. I would have to show up at her doorstep and hope she would talk to me, a prospect I didn't relish. But first I had to go to the County Clerk's office to look up the deed.

The county offices are in one of the most attractive buildings in Clinton Falls. It is at the foot of Main Street, a sprawling red brick colonial affair trimmed in white that looks better to me every year, especially when I see buildings in colors like turquoise, peach, and salmon that have sprouted up in the suburbs. During our winters (Clinton Falls averages 154 inches of snow annually), those buildings look as out of place in the snow as a dowager would wearing a full-length fur coat on a tropical beach.

I went to the County Clerk's office first to look in the Deed Book, and then to the Property Tax Office. Everything was in order. Geneva Stratton held full title to the property at 1801 Main Street. Her latest tax bill was over twelve thousand dollars, a hefty sum to pay on an empty building. According to the clerk, a friendly, talkative woman, Geneva Stratton has appealed her tax assessment every year.

It was almost eleven o'clock when I left the county building. I was just a few minutes away from Geneva Stratton's. Although I would have liked to put off calling on her, I pushed myself to do it. The weather was so lovely that it seemed like a guarantee of success: I would convince Geneva Stratton to let me have an option on her property because nothing could happen to spoil this perfect day.

The buildings on the block that Avery Laird bought were deteriorating, the storefronts all boarded-up, the paint peeling, the mortar crumbling. The next block, however, was bustling with activity. A new Central New York Bank building was going up, the largest, tallest office building ever to be constructed in Clinton Falls. The mayor, Ernie Boldt, who was in Buddy's graduating class in high school, took every opportunity he could to link the new building with what he called a "Renaissance for downtown." As I walked up to Geneva Stratton's building, I began to wonder when Avery Laird started to buy up the block. I also wondered if he was on the board of the Central New York Bank.

Commercial buildings don't have doorbells. If she were there, Geneva Stratton would be in the apartment over the store, so I had to bang loudly if I wanted her to hear me. I took off my shoe and gave the boards covering the glass door a couple of solid whacks. Above, a window opened. "Who's there?" a stern voice demanded.

I put my shoe on and went to the curb so she could see me, glad that the clothes I was wearing, a khaki skirt and yellow blouse, were simple and unassuming. The messages that clothing sends was not the least of the lessons I learned selling real estate. "My name is Ginger Middleton," I said. "I'd like to talk to you, Mrs. Stratton. I think I can help you."

Both the window and the screen were so dirty that I could barely see her. "If I want help, I'll ask for it!" she said, putting her hands on the window to lower it.

"I believe I can get you a price that you'll accept from Avery Laird. Just give me a few minutes, please."

That was another lesson I learned in real estate: tell people what they want to hear, no matter how impossible it is, to lure them in. Once they nibble at the bait, most are easy to hook.

Mrs. Stratton, however, was an exception. "What did you say your name is?" she said, her hands still on the window.

"Ginger Middleton."

"Who do you work for?"

"Myself."

"Are you a realtor?"

"I was," I said, "but I retired."

"Then what's your angle?"

Shielding my eyes, I squinted up at the shadowy figure behind the screen. "I'm really not comfortable discussing this while standing at the edge of the curb," I said. "I don't think the street is an appropriate place to do business."

She didn't reply. But she didn't close the window, either.

I moved toward the building, out of the sun. It wasn't long before the lock on the door clicked. "Well, come in then," Mrs. Stratton said, motioning me inside.

The store had a haunted look, long empty aisles between dusty display counters, some of them still holding odd pieces of merchandise—yellowed cards of buttons, crumbling packages of balloons, birthday candles, bobby pins, paper doilies in torn cellophane packages, bottles of dried-up shoe polish, party favors, accordion-pleated plastic rain bonnets, a bald doll missing an eye. Only the aisle that led directly to the back of the store had been walked on recently; the remainder of the black-and-white-checkerboard floor was covered with a coat of gray grime. "I can't use the back entrance anymore," Mrs. Stratton said, bolting the door. "The bums have turned the side and back alleys into toilets. It's a disgrace! And there are so many of them now, not just a few winos like it was years ago. Some nights there are a couple dozen people down there peeing and sleeping and doing God knows what! The police don't do anything about it. I guess they feel they don't have to because I'm the only one left living decent on this block. Everyone else is gone, all sold out."

Geneva Stratton's frustration showed clearly in her face. Her eyes, small and dark, shone with indignation, and her sharp chin quivered with anger.

She's a short woman, about five feet tall I'd guess, solidly built, and surprisingly unwrinkled though she must be in her late sixties or early seventies, at least. That day she had on a simple cotton-print dress, worn but clean, the style and type of which my mother used to call a house dress. "It's difficult," I said. "So many people are homeless today, and there is no place for them to go."

"Some of them never held a job!" she said emphatically.

I wasn't about to argue. Above all I needed to win Mrs. Stratton's confidence, which I couldn't do by disagreeing with her. "I'd like to talk to you about getting an offer that you'd accept from Avery Laird. Is there a place where we could sit down?"

She looked me over carefully, as if I were a piece of merchandise that she was considering buying. "What do you get out of it?"

I had hoped to establish a rapport with her, to make her feel comfortable with me so that I could begin building her trust. Geneva Stratton, however, is anything but a trusting woman. As I soon learned, she's had hard experiences in her life, and she's buried every one of them deep inside her, as if storing them in a well from which she draws sustenance. I had never met anyone so angry and bitter. Perhaps the energy of those emotions is what has kept her face unlined.

She nodded to herself, as if my hesitation confirmed her worst suspicions. "Your angle," she said, her eyes even brighter than before, "what's your angle?"

"I want something from Avery Laird that he isn't

willing to give. You have something he wants. I'm willing to use my skills to help you so that I get what I want."

"What is it that you want?"

"An interview," I said. "I want to write an article about him for a magazine."

She frowned. "An interview?" she said, as though she hadn't heard me correctly. "You're not looking for money?"

"No."

"Well," she said, "maybe we can talk."

I followed her through the store and an empty back storage room to a sagging wooden staircase that led upstairs. Green paint was flaking off the walls, and a long yellowed water stain snaked along the ceiling in the upstairs hall. The door to the apartment opened directly into the kitchen; it was clean, but everything was so ancient that I felt like I had stepped into a movie set. With the exception of the refrigerator, everything in the room—the gas stove, the glass-front cupboards, the worn linoleum counter tops, the yellow Formica-top table and chrome chairs—had to be at least fifty years old. The floor was so worn that I couldn't tell what color it had been. "Have a seat," she said.

I took a chair opposite hers. What was left of the stuffing in the seat was compressed to conform to someone else's body; it felt like an uneven board. "You might as well know straight off that I don't intend to sell to Laird. I'm going to hold out as long as I can."

"Why?" I asked. "Isn't it dangerous, as well as lonely, being the only resident on the block?"

"He wrecked this block!" she said. "He hurt every business on it when he built that Sunrise Mall. It wasn't just businesses that he hurt, either. He wrecked people's lives! Ed Johnson, the fellow who owned Miss Muffet's, the children's store, committed suicide after he went bankrupt. The Langmeyers lost everything they had when their hardware business went under. When our business fell off, my husband couldn't sleep nights. He'd get up and he'd go downstairs and pace. He'd walk up and down the aisles, up and down, up and down, all night. One morning I found him down there in the aisle by the scissors and stationery supplies. He was stone cold. A heart attack."

"I'm sorry," I said.

"His insurance is what has kept me here. Otherwise I'd be out on the street like Alma Ridgeway. The Ridgeway's owned a shoe store called..." She paused, pursing her lips as she prodded her memory for the name.

"The Bootery," I supplied.

She nodded. "Then you knew the store."

"I knew all the stores, including yours. I was born and raised in Clinton Falls. Except for a very brief time, I've lived here all my life."

"Then you know what a scoundrel Avery Laird is! When he started buying up this block, no one knew it was him. Some fellow came around, said he represented a real estate group—I forget the name. Avery Laird's no group! He just hid behind a name! I told the reporter from the newspaper about that, but he didn't put it in the article. No one's got the guts to stand up to Avery Laird except me!"

"I do," I said, cutting her off. Mrs. Stratton is a talker, and it had become obvious that she hadn't had an opportunity to vent her anger against Avery Laird for a while, probably since she had talked to the reporter. I realized that I was in danger of becoming her captive audience if I didn't take charge. "What will you accept for this property?" I asked. "The bottom line?"

"There is no bottom line! I won't sell to Laird! Never! After what he's done..."

"I hope you realize that you're going to be forced to sell," I said, interrupting her.

"He can't force me to do anything! This is my property, and as long as I pay the taxes on it, it's mine!"

Mrs. Stratton's face turned a deep, angry red. For a moment I hesitated, afraid that if I pushed on she might have a stroke. But the alternative was leaving empty-handed. At least I could educate her. "He can't force you directly," I said. "What he can do, however, is make it difficult and expensive for you to remain here."

"What do you mean?" she demanded, her color not quite as high.

"He can exert pressure on the city to have this building inspected—the plumbing, the wiring, the roof, the gutters. You'd have to correct every violation, perhaps pay fines as well. I noticed a water stain on the ceiling in the upstairs hall. It could end up costing you thousands of dollars by the time you find the source of the leak and repair it. Repairs on commercial buildings are expensive. Are you willing to put a lot of money into this building just to fight

Avery Laird?"

Mrs. Stratton clasped her hands together. Again, I noticed how old and worn her dress was, nearly as old and worn-looking as the things in the kitchen. "How much has he offered you?" I asked gently, realizing what holding onto the building had cost her.

"Ninety thousand," she said bitterly.

"What would you accept?"

"The property is assessed for two-hundred-sixty-seven thousand. Then there's the taxes I've paid." She thought for a moment. "Two-hundred-seventy-five thousand would do it."

She eyed me suspiciously. "What's in it for you? What's your cut?"

"Nothing," I said. "I already told you: I'm not interested in making money on this. Instead, I want him to give me an interview."

"How are you going to get him to do it?"

"I'll buy an option from you that will give me the exclusive right for the next twelve months to sell this property. Then I'll contact him and offer to let him buy the option from me, providing he gives me the interview."

"What if he refuses?"

"He loses a year," I said, "and you're protected. He won't bother you because I'm the only one who can sell to him."

"You said you'd buy that option from me. What will you pay for it?"

"Just a token amount," I said, "maybe ten dollars."

Mrs. Stratton's eyes gleamed. "Don't options usually go for much more, like five or ten thousand dollars?"

"Yes," I said. "But someone who pays that kind of money is counting on making a profit. I'm not going to make any money selling your property. I'll be working for nothing."

"You're getting something you want," she said in a tone that let me know I'd stung her pride.

"You're right," I said, extending my hand, "I am getting what I want, or at least a chance at it. Do we have a deal?"

She grasped my hand. Her grip was strong. "It's a deal," she said.

After I left Geneva Stratton's, I drove to the Diamond Real Estate office I had worked out of for seven years. It's in an older suburb north of town, less than five minutes from our house. Diamond Real Estate does the largest volume of residential business in the county. It's owned by Earl Diamond, a man of few morals and fewer scruples. Over the years I've heard so many stories about Earl that nothing anyone could tell me about him would surprise me. Earl Diamond would do anything, absolutely anything, to make a buck.

Fortunately, it was lunch time so the office was empty except for the secretary, Lucy, and a couple of agents on the phones. Lucy greeted me with a warm smile. "It's great to see you," she said. "Are you bored with retirement and ready to come back?"

"Not quite," I said. "How are things going around here? I understand the market hasn't reached a bottom yet."

"It's slow," she said quietly, tilting her head toward the back office to indicate that Earl was in. It's an unwritten rule at Diamond Real Estate that business is always spoken of as being up, no matter what the actual conditions. "What brings you here?"

"I want to check a form for a friend of mine," I said. "Is all that stuff still kept in the black filing cabinet?"

"Yes," she said, reaching to pick up the ringing telephone. I went directly to the filing cabinet where the forms are kept, nodding at the agents who were on the phones as I passed their desks. Quickly, I hunted through the file drawer for the forms, found the one I wanted, and slipped it into my purse. I was halfway to the door when I heard Earl's nasal voice. "Ginger, is that you?"

I stopped and turned. "In the flesh," I said, forcing a smile.

Earl hurried toward me, his head characteristically thrust forward. He looks like a rooster: he has a shock of red hair, a beak of a nose, and the longest, skinniest neck I've ever seen. His head is constantly in motion, as if he's afraid he's going to miss something. "Have you had enough of retirement?" he said, extending his hand.

"Whoa," I said, "not so fast."

"The sooner you plunge in, the better. In a few weeks you'll feel like you never left."

"I have been getting itchy."

Earl smiled broadly, revealing a yellowed over bite. "Great news! I'll tell Lucy to put you on the schedule for floor duty."

I tried not to shudder at the thought. "I'm not quite ready yet."

Earl frowned, clearly displeased. "You're a great

producer, Ginger. It's a sin to waste a talent like yours. I can't let you."

What you really mean is that it's a sin I'm not working seventy hours a week, putting money in your pocket, I thought. "Earl, you'll be the first to know when I decide to come back. I promise."

I gave him the brightest smile I could muster. Then I told him how much I'd enjoyed seeing him, mumbled something about an appointment and hurried away, praying he wouldn't pursue me. I waved to Lucy as I sailed out the front door. My breathing didn't return to normal until I turned the key in the ignition.

During dinner, I told Buddy about Geneva Stratton. We had eggplant Parmesan, one of Buddy's favorites. He's crazy about Italian food, especially anything that has a combination of tomato and cheese. "I typed the option this afternoon," I said. "It's ready for her to sign."

"You might want to have a lawyer check it over first," he said.

"Why?"

"You're playing in the big leagues. If there are any weaknesses in your option, even one, you can be sure Laird's lawyers will find it."

"It's a form Earl has been using for years; he probably got it from a lawyer in the first place. Earl wouldn't use a contract that wasn't airtight and slanted in his favor. He's the greediest man I've ever known. All I had to do was fill in names, numbers, and dates."

Buddy leaned back in his chair and looked at me thoughtfully. I noticed shadows under his eyes. He puts in long days during the football season. "Are you going after the Laird interview for the sheer challenge of it, or are you really sincere about trying your hand at journalism?"

"Both," I said.

"If your plan works, your career will begin with a flying start."

"What could be better?"

"Spectacular beginnings sometimes have a way of fizzling out."

"I'll take my chances," I said. "Besides, if it works, I owe some of this spectacular beginning to you."

"Me?"

"Don't you remember? You came up with the suggestion to interview Avery Laird at the Thackers' party."

"I just threw Laird's name out so that editor wouldn't bother me."

"Well, I caught it," I said.

It hurts to remember what Buddy said then: "I hope I'm not going to wish I'd kept my mouth shut."

IV

Getting through to Avery Laird was as frustrating as opening a trick box which has other boxes nested inside, so that one keeps opening box after box, getting nowhere. The first person I spoke to at Laird Enterprises was a general receptionist. I had to explain who I was and why I was calling before she connected me to Avery Laird's office. Then I had to repeat the same information to his receptionist, who transferred me to his secretary. Again, like a refrain, I had to repeat who I was and why I was calling. At that point I was so irritated I had all I could do to keep my voice modulated.

Modulation didn't help. His secretary asked me for my telephone number and told me that she would have one of Mr. Laird's attorneys contact me.

That did it! "What is your name, please?" I said.

"Ms. Evans," she said.

"Ms. Evans, you may give Mr. Laird the following message: I have an option on 1801 Main Street that I will sell to him if we can agree upon terms. I will not—I repeat, I will not—deal with anyone but him."

I gave her my telephone number and spelled my

last name before hanging up.

Within an hour I was contacted by a fellow who said he worked for the Oakton Corporation. "I understand you have an option on 1801 Main Street," he said.

"Yes," I said. "And since you also understand English, I'll give you the same message I've already given to more people at Laird Enterprises than I care to count: I will not discuss the option with anyone except Avery Laird."

I hung up without saying good-by.

The next call came from one of Avery Laird's attorneys, who coolly informed me that Avery Laird does not become personally involved in any property acquisitions made by Laird Enterprises. "All acquisitions are handled by Mr. Laird's representatives," he said.

"Then Mr. Laird will not be acquiring the property at 1801 Main Street," I said.

I don't know if lawyers in general are so accustomed to being treated badly that they develop the ability to hold people on the line against their wills or if it was this attorney's particular talent, but he was so skillful that I found myself arguing with him. Each time I started to hang up he forged ahead, saying something provocative that I couldn't ignore. Finally, I caught on. Rather than responding to him, I simply said, "My option is for a year. When the year expires, I will renew it for another year. And then another year. Perhaps three or four years will be sufficient time for Mr. Laird to reconsider his policy concerning acquisitions!"

I slammed the receiver down before he could

respond.

Several days later another Laird attorney called. When I took the option to Geneva Stratton for her to sign, I asked her to let me know if she was contacted by Laird's people. She had called me the day before, so I was prepared. "You've checked out the option and know that it's valid," I said. "You also know that I'm not willing to deal with anyone but Mr. Laird. If I'm called again by anyone connected with Laird Enterprises other than Mr. Laird, I'll consider it harassment."

Then I waited. A week passed, and then another. I tried to keep busy, which wasn't easy. I'm not into gardening or sewing, and although I like a clean house, I'm not one of those women who gets an inner glow from scrubbing down the kitchen walls. Besides, I had gone through every closet and cupboard after I quit selling real estate. I did give Zack's room a thorough going-over, and straightened some closets that needed it, but after I was done there was nothing left to do but read. Or shop, play tennis or bridge, and meet friends for lunch.

The longer I waited, the more important Avery Laird's call became. I felt as if I were waiting for a new phase of my life to begin. I'd hated real estate— the hours, the cut-throat competitiveness, the interminable days I'd had to spend with people whom I couldn't stand, carting them around. The day I quit I had spent close to seven hours with a couple from out of town who had their two sons, ages five and seven, with them. All day the children fought and whined and nagged, until the sound of their voices made my head pound. They left their dirty fingerprints on the windows and walls of the houses they went through; they opened people's drawers and cupboards while their parents looked away benignly, as though the boys didn't belong to them. The younger child picked his nose incessantly and then managed to touch nearly everything he came in contact with. I gagged when I saw him running his hands along people's kitchen counters. Several times I tactfully suggested that the boys might be happier if they could relax and watch television in their hotel room with one parent while I showed houses to the other parent. Simultaneously both parents assured me that they would stay together, so they "...could find the perfect house as a family." In other words, neither one of them wanted to be alone with the monsters they created.

Late in the afternoon, after we stopped for hot dogs and French fries, which the monsters insisted they had to have—just as they'd had to have pizza and ice cream and soft drinks and hamburgers on earlier stops—the oldest boy, who was so hyperactive that I didn't once see him sit still, even to eat, vomited all over the back seat and floor of my car. Then, as if not to be outdone, his younger brother followed his example. Their mother, an anxious-looking blond who had a nervous smile, was sitting between them. As far as I was concerned, she got what she deserved.

The car was less than a month old, a brand-new gray Honda Accord. I scrubbed and scrubbed but wasn't able to get the smell out completely, so I had to have the carpet and the upholstery on the back seat replaced.

It wasn't the damage to the car that made me quit. Gum, candy, and ice cream had been left on the seats and carpet of the car I had traded in for the Honda. And I had lost count of the inconsiderate adults who had stepped into my car without wiping their muddy shoes after walking on construction sites.

Something inside me snapped when those nasty children vomited. I knew that I could never again spend another day with strangers, showing them houses. I could never again hustle to get a listing. I could never again work out of an office with agents that I didn't trust, people who would steal my clients and customers if they could.

I chose real estate because it was easy to get into and it had a lot of potential. I got my license and began working for Diamond Real Estate the year Steve started at the University of Michigan. Although we didn't need money for Steve because of his scholarships, we figured we would need it for Zack. At the time, our house needed immediate work that we couldn't afford to have done on Buddy's income: a new roof, gutters, furnace, and kitchen floor. The family room furniture and carpeting were badly worn, and the drapes and carpeting in the living room needed to be replaced as well. The shabbiness of our home had long bothered me, but both Buddy and I felt that it was important for me to be a stay-at-home mother while our boys were growing up. We didn't want Steve and Zack raising themselves.

So there were plenty of reasons for me to go to work besides the most important one: I was ready. After spending almost twenty years at home, I wanted to go out into the world and achieve something. At the time, Buddy said, "Be careful. The world isn't as nice a place as you imagine it is."

He was right. During my first few months at Diamond Real Estate, other agents listened in on my telephone conversations and looked through my appointment book, then called my prospects before I caught on. When I complained to Earl Diamond, his only comment was, "You're in a competitive business."

I probably would have quit if my father hadn't died unexpectedly of a stroke. It was a devastating blow; he had just celebrated his seventieth birthday. I took time off from work, more for my mother than for myself. She'd always been a self-sufficient, capable woman, but with my father gone, she seemed barely able to function. After she'd stayed with us for about a month, Buddy asked me one night as we were getting ready for bed when I thought she'd be leaving. "I don't know," I said.

"Steve will be coming home for Thanksgiving in a couple of weeks," he said.

"He can sleep in Zack's room."

"I want you to understand something," Buddy said, resting his hands on my shoulders. "If we put Steve in Zack's room, your mother will never leave. She'll stay here for the rest of her life. She looks like she's slipped into a state of permanent mourning. I've been in funeral parlors that are more cheerful than this house. At least Zack and I can escape during the day, but you're stuck here. I feel sorry for your mother, but I'm going to feel sorrier for you if you don't get her back into her own house."

What he'd said was true, but I didn't see how I could nudge her back into her own home. The impact of my father's death seemed to have crushed the life out of her. My mother has always had a quiet, gentle nature, unlike my father, who was extroverted and temperamental, certainly not an easy man. My parents complimented each other perfectly: my father drew my mother out, and she, unflappable, calmed and steadied him like the ballast on a ship. Without him she simply sat, hour upon hour, speaking only when someone spoke to her. "She's still in shock," I said.

"Maybe getting her back into her own house will get her out of it."

"What will I tell her?" I said, feeling vulnerable. I had just lost my father. I couldn't bear the thought of hurting her.

"You could remind her that Steve will be coming home. You could also tell her that you feel you have to get back to work."

"She knows I haven't sold any houses. She also knows that most of my leads were stolen from me."

"Tell her you feel that if you don't go back soon, you'll lose your drive and give up."

I was awake most of the night. Although I agreed with Buddy—eventually my mother did have to pick up her life—I didn't think she should be pushed. As I listened to his deep, even breathing, I thought of his mother. She died when he was eighteen, and over the years he's turned her into a saint. Eve Middleton was a nice woman, but she wasn't the paragon Buddy has made her out to be. I know that if the situation were reversed, if it were his mother, he'd let her stay forever.

At dawn I decided to do it Buddy's way because it was easier than arguing with him. But I resented his lack of patience for a long time afterward.

Taking my mother back to her own house was one of the hardest things I've ever done. She looked so lost and pale and small. My father's death had made a terrible hole in our lives, both hers and mine, but for her it was a chasm. I had to choke back tears when we entered the sprawling white clapboard house where I grew up and where she'd lived nearly all her married life. I could see my father in every room—talking, laughing, full of life—and I knew that she could, too. But she's a brave woman, my mother. She looked up at me with steady gray eyes and said, "I'll be fine."

I heard a quaver of age in her voice and couldn't speak. I could only nod.

She was fine. With time she slowly adjusted. And I plunged back into selling real estate and worked off my grief.

Sometimes I think about the timing of my father's death, that if he hadn't died when he did I might have quit real estate because I had a poor start. If I had quit, I might never have learned that besides inheriting his height and ease with people, I also inherited my father's ability to sell.

My last year in real estate I made well over one hundred thousand dollars, more than double Buddy's combined coaching and teaching salaries. It was big money, but it didn't come easily: I earned it. I worked every day, seven days a week, except when we were on vacation. Our dinner hour, which had always been a high point in our family life, became haphazard, often takeout food eaten at irregular hours. Although Zack didn't mind having pizza several times a week, he did mind my erratic hours and the telephone calls that interrupted our meals, evenings, and weekends. After I noticed the skin around his eyes tighten with irritation when the telephone rang while we were eating, I let the answering machine take calls during meals.

Most of my clients and customers were pleasant to work with, not like the couple who had the two monster sons. But constantly running from house to house, developing new leads, presenting offers on evenings when I should have been home with Buddy and Zack, and the incessant telephone calls all took their toll. I had earned the money to fix the house, send Zack to Cornell, and to help Steve with law school. Enough was enough.

If the fact that I earned so much more than he did bothered Buddy, he never mentioned it, so neither did I. But it did bother me. Somehow it just didn't seem right.

Within weeks after I quit, time began to drag. Most of my friends work; the few that don't, like Jane Thacker, are involved in community work. I read the want ads and found nothing: either I wasn't qualified or I didn't want the job. I began to feel as uneasy as I did when I was a child and adults asked me what I wanted to be when I grew up. Then I happened to see an ad looking for an experienced proofreader, which made me think of writing. The more I thought about it, the more I wanted to give it a try, but I knew no one would hire me. And I didn't want to send out articles that would be rejected. I needed a solid opportunity and thought that I'd found it until almost four weeks passed and Avery Laird still hadn't called.

On a dismal Friday morning I had just gone out

the door to go grocery shopping when the telephone rang. I probably wouldn't have come back in if I hadn't decided to put on a raincoat. I answered the phone on the third ring. It was Avery Laird.

His voice was cool, his manner brusque. He wanted to know if I could meet with him at eleven forty-five on Monday in his office.

I hesitated, thinking that the time he had picked, just before lunch, meant that he intended to give me a fast shuffle. But then I realized my proposal wouldn't take more than a few minutes, so the time was irrelevant. "Yes," I said, "eleven forty-five will be fine."

V

All weekend I told myself not to think about my appointment with Avery Laird, which was as effective as telling someone on a diet not to think about food. I must have imagined the meeting, with every possible objection he could make to my proposal, and every argument I could use to overcome his objections, until I was positive that no reaction he could conceivably have would surprise me.

I was wrong. He did surprise me.

If I'd had more to keep me busy over the weekend, I probably wouldn't have been so over prepared. Buddy isn't around much on weekends during the football season. There is a game every Friday night and a five-hour team meeting that takes a large chunk out of Sunday. On Saturday and Sunday mornings he plays tennis; he cuts the grass on Saturday afternoon. I met Jane for lunch on Saturday, and Buddy and I went out to dinner with old friends on Saturday night. The rest of the time I was alone, even when Buddy was home.

Buddy's team lost Friday night. The loss affected our entire weekend, as a loss always does. Buddy played fierce tennis Saturday and Sunday; however, winning every set wasn't enough. He was quieter than usual, and Sunday night he sat and brooded, mentally replaying the game. He didn't say more than a few words to me all evening. On Monday morning he left for school early, probably to prepare a new practice plan. "Aren't you going to wish me luck?" I asked as he started out the door.

"Luck?" He turned and looked at me, as if he expected to see an explanation stuck to my forehead.

"Never mind," I said.

Then he remembered and gave me an abashed grin. "Sorry, I forgot that your meeting is today," he said. "Hit a homer."

He waved before shutting the door. I didn't wave back.

The Laird offices are located in an unpretentious two-story sand-colored brick building that is a few minutes away from the Sunrise Mall. After I parked the car, I glanced in the rear-view mirror for a last-minute check to make sure that everything was in place. I wore a well-cut gray wool suit and a turquoise-and-gray paisley blouse. Several copies of the option to Geneva Stratton's property were in a new manila envelope.

Everything inside the building is modern—all white and various shades of gray, with a lot of stainless steel and glass—a cool, if not chilly, atmosphere. I was immediately directed to Avery Laird's office on the second floor, where I was greeted by Ms. Evans, the woman whom I had wanted to throttle when I had spoken to her the month before.

She was as interested in me as I was in her, although both of us hid our curiosity well. Ms. Evans is around my age, an attractive redhead though a bit hard looking. She had on too much make-up, as well as too much jewelry: a glittery starfish-shaped pin on her green dress, large earrings, and rings on almost all her fingers. I noticed that she was wearing high-heeled sling-back shoes that were more appropriate for a nightclub than an office, and wondered if her relationship with Avery Laird extended beyond business. Her manner, however, was most efficient. "Mr. Laird is tied up on a long distance call. He should be with you shortly."

In less than five minutes she ushered me into his office.

I already knew that Avery Laird was in his fifties. He's approximately the same height as Buddy but has a smaller frame. I hope I didn't look as surprised as I felt. Maybe it was his custom-tailored suit or his small, impeccably-groomed mustache or his black hair, which is graying at the temples. Whatever it was, I didn't expect such an elegant-looking man.

He rose from behind his desk, which had a black base and a glass top at least an inch thick, and extended his hand. "Mrs. Middleton," he said.

His hand was cool and dry. He gestured for me to sit down on one of the black leather chairs in front of the desk. After I was settled, I opened the manila envelope and handed him a copy of the option. He scanned it quickly, pausing in several places where I knew the agreement was so tightly written that it would be impossible to break. "How much do you want?" he said, leaning back in his chair. He tossed the option on the desk.

"Two hundred seventy-five thousand dollars plus an interview," I said. "The sale is contingent on the interview."

He sat straight up. "What do you mean by *interview*?"

"I am not going to make any money on the option. Geneva Stratton will get the entire two hundred seventy-five thousand. My only interest is in interviewing you for a magazine article."

His eyes narrowed. "What magazine?"

"I hope to place the article in *Forum*."

"You *hope to place*," he repeated, as if he weren't sure he'd heard me correctly.

Over the weekend I had debated whether I should give the impression that *Forum* had already agreed to publish the article, or to be honest and forthright. I've never been able to lie very well, so I decided that honesty was my only choice. I briefly told him about my degree in journalism and my desire to try to write after so many years. "I happened to learn that *Forum* is very interested in publishing an article about you," I explained. "Then I heard about Geneva Stratton's property..."

To my amazement, he started to laugh. I didn't know how to react. My skin prickled with embarrassment. Somehow I managed a slight smile.

"Forgive me," he said. "I wasn't laughing at you. If anything, I was laughing at myself. For weeks I've wondered about your angle, exactly what it was that you wanted. I thought I had some pretty good ideas, but I never expected anything like this."

"I hope my proposal will be good for more than a

laugh."

"Two hundred seventy-five thousand is a steep price for Mrs. Stratton's property," he said.

"Perhaps," I said, "but she won't accept less. She's a stubborn woman. She'll hold on as long as she has to, and every day she stays there, you're paying taxes on property you can't develop."

He nodded, acknowledging the point I'd made. "I could make it difficult for her," he said in a measured tone.

"Yes," I agreed. "But if you do, you're leaving yourself open for a lot of negative publicity. Now that she's learned how effective it is, she could take her troubles to the newspaper."

He sat back in his chair and studied me as if I were a chess piece he was contemplating moving. It struck me that his eyes, which are deep-set, are nearly the same shade of green as new money. "You have a deal," he said finally. "I'll buy the option at your price."

"I'll be happy to sell it to you upon the completion of a successful interview."

"What do you mean by *a successful interview*? I can't guarantee that you're going to like what I say."

"Whether I like or dislike what you say is irrelevant. You're entitled to your views, whatever they are," I said. "By *successful* I mean that you'll give me a decent amount of time and answer my questions thoughtfully. If you make a joke out of it, or say 'no comment' to most of what I ask, then it will be a sham and the deal will be off."

He looked at his watch. "It's after twelve. I have a meeting at one thirty. Would you like to join me for lunch? Perhaps you can give me an idea of the kinds of questions you'll ask."

"Uh...sure," I said, so taken aback that I wondered later if I looked as surprised as I felt.

He suggested that we eat at Treehaven, the oldest and most exclusive country club in Clinton Falls. There is only one other country club in the area, The Fairways, which is relatively new and considerably further from town; it was started by people who couldn't get into Treehaven. We drove in separate cars. He has a black Mercedes.

Treehaven is just a mile or so from his office in an area that was once farmland but is now all built up. Buddy learned how to play tennis and golf there. His parents were members for years, but they never used the place except for the dining room. Buddy's father's sole interest in life was his business; nothing else mattered to him, including Buddy.

The main dining room at Treehaven has the look of old money: a polished wood floor, worn oriental rugs, good china and silver. We were seated at a window that overlooked the golf course. The view was lovely, meticulously-kept rolling turf rimmed in the distance by trees in autumn colors.

"Treehaven old timers still occasionally talk about some of the tennis matches your husband played here when he was young. They think he had the potential to be a ranking professional," he said after a waitress, who looked nearly as old as the country club, took our order.

"Baseball was my husband's sport," I said, wondering how much he knew about me, and apparently Buddy as well.

"I understand he played professionally."

"Briefly," I said, disliking the direction in which the conversation was going. "Have you ever been interviewed?"

"Once. Something I said was taken out of context, so I've avoided interviews ever since," he said, adding with a smile, "until now."

"I won't take anything out of context. It isn't fair. But I will ask you a wide range of questions, everything from what your present projects are to how you think the people in the community perceive you."

"Hmmm," he said, "I wonder. How do you perceive me?"

"I don't know yet," I said, laughing.

During lunch he asked my opinion about a recently developed plaza that was rumored to be close to bankruptcy. Despite my efforts to swing back to his interview, he skillfully kept the conversation on real estate. It was both flattering and frustrating, because he listened intently—almost the way Zack does, with his head tilted to one side—to everything I had to say. "Why did you stop selling real estate?" he asked.

"I'd had enough," I said, putting down my fork. "Maybe someday I'll tell you about some of my clients. Now, however, I'd appreciate it if you'd tell my how much you know about me."

His eyebrows rose. "Why do you ask?"

"It's obvious that you've done your homework."

He pushed his plate aside. "People often try to approach me with various deals. I pay my staff well to screen them. It's a matter of self-protection: there are a lot of hucksters around."

"You still haven't answered my question: what do

you know about me?"

I saw what I believe was a flicker of respect in his eyes. "You worked for Diamond Real Estate and you were quite successful," he said. "Actually, I know more about your husband and your sons, particularly your oldest son, because I read the sports section of the newspaper. I remember when your son was injured. It was a tragedy."

"No," I said. "A tragedy is a senseless death or a calamity or a disaster. Or it could be the destruction of something precious and irreplaceable. My son is going to have a wonderful life, probably a better one than he would have had if he'd played professional football. He'll be graduating from Harvard Law School in the spring. He'll have a long, successful career that won't be over when he's in his thirties."

"Still, giving up all that potential money and glory had to be hard."

"Steve never mentions it. He's gotten on with his life."

Avery (we were on a first-name basis at that point) wanted his lawyers to draw up a Letter of Agreement which would cover the option and the interview. "I would prefer to have my attorney draw up the Agreement," I said.

"It will be an additional expense for you, and you aren't making any money as it is."

"I'll be compensated for the article."

"*Forum* can't pay very much. It's upscale, but it's a regional magazine. Its circulation isn't that big."

"If the interview goes well, perhaps your lawyers will prepare an assignment of the option."

"You have a deal," he said.

We shook hands. Perhaps it was my imagination, but it seemed to me that he held my hand a little longer than necessary.

I drove home elated. I couldn't wait to call Neil Hamilton to ask him to draft a Letter of Agreement. The telephone was ringing when I walked in. It was Jane. "Thank God you're home," she said. "I'm coming over."

"Is something wrong?"

"Everything is," she said.

In all the years I'd known Jane, I'd never heard her sound so upset, as though something horrible had happened. I decided to call Neil Hamilton's office first. If I had time, I'd change afterward.

Neil was free, so I talked to him about the Letter of Agreement. First, however, I thanked him for setting me on the course that helped me get the interview. "You did it all yourself," he said. "I didn't have a hand in it."

"Yes, you did," I said. "You made me realize that an opportunity could exist but that it was up to me to find it."

"And you struck gold," he said, laughing.

We briefly discussed the Letter of Agreement. I told him that I wanted it to be as binding as possible. Although Avery Laird had been pleasant, that didn't mean I trusted him. Neil told me it would be ready on Wednesday. Then he hesitated, as though he were going to say something and decided against it.

Jane arrived before I had time to wonder about Neil's hesitation. She must have driven considerably over the speed limit; I didn't expect her for at least another five minutes. She looked awful. Her eyes were puffy and swollen, and her skin had a dreadful greenish tinge, as though she were seriously ill. "What's happened?" I asked.

"Oh, Ginger," she said. Then she started to sob.

I put my arms around her; she felt surprisingly fragile. I realized that I had never seen her cry, not even when her mother died. "I... have... to... stop... this," she said between sobs.

"Can I make you a cup of tea? I have some herbal tea, chamomile. It's very soothing."

"I've... been... throwing up... since... yesterday," she said. "I can't... keep... anything ...down."

"I'll make some anyway," I said, feeling the need to be doing something. The state Jane was in really unsettled me. In the twenty-five years I'd known her, I'd seen her handle every crisis that came her way with a calm, clear-eyed practicality that I'd always envied.

She followed me into the kitchen and sighed as she sank onto a chair at the table. After I put the water on to boil, I sat opposite her. I didn't know what to say. She took a tissue from her purse and blew her nose. "Cal wants a divorce," she said, her eyes filling with tears again. She took a deep breath and let it out slowly. "He told me yesterday. He's been seeing her for over a year. She works in the office in the Syracuse store. Her name is Lianne. She's twenty-three years old! He has a daughter who's older than she is! He even had the gall to show me her picture. He handed it to me like it was a trophy. You should have seen him standing there all puffed up like a bloated fish! He looked so foolish, a fifty-two-year-old man proud of himself because a female younger than his daughter will go to bed with him.

"Over the years, I occasionally suspected that he was cheating on me, but I never had proof. Maybe I just didn't want to know. I come from a broken family, and I didn't want that for my daughters."

"I thought your mother was a widow."

"My parents were divorced a year before my father died. Divorce wasn't as common then as it is today. I was twelve years old, a brutal age to have your family fall apart. At the time I vowed that I would do anything to avoid a divorce if I ever got married and had children."

That certainly explained why she was always so incredibly patient with Cal. "How did your father die?" I asked.

"In a plane crash," she said. "I only saw him twice in the six months prior to his death. He and my mother had been fighting over some property. I remember feeling so lost and cheated. A part of me never forgave her," she said, stifling a sob. "Cal wants the house! Can you believe it! I put my heart and soul into that place, and he wants to romp around in it with her. I think he imagines himself with her in the master bathroom, probably playing in the jacuzzi. He's fixated on that bathroom. It's as if all that marble shouts his success.

"Damn him!" she said. "I picked out everything in the bathroom, in all the rooms. I spent a year of my life on that house. If I hadn't worked so hard on it, I might have realized that he was having an affair."

"What would you have done?"

"I would have figured out how to handle it somehow," she said. "Cal's like a child, easily distracted."

Steam spouted from the kettle. I got up to make the tea. When I brought it back to the table, Jane gently moved her cup and saucer aside. "Have you eaten anything?"

"I can't even keep water down."

"Maybe you should call the doctor."

"There isn't a pill in the world for what's happened to me," she said. "I'm going to be fifty years old in a few months. *Fifty*. I realize that I'm far from being the first woman who has had this happen to her, but I tried so hard. And now it's all so bitter to swallow."

She bit her bottom lip to stop herself from sobbing again. "Cal had the nerve to suggest that I accept a lower than customary settlement because business has been down lately." She leaned forward. "I've never told this to anyone, *not anyone*: the idea to discount the appliances wasn't Cal's. It was mine. In fact, I left the girls here with you the day I went to the store to tell him what to do. We were so broke that I didn't have the money to pay a sitter for a couple of hours; we were just a hair away from bankruptcy. I went over the invoices and figured out what we could sell the inventory for and still manage to stay afloat. I wrote down the prices and told him that I was going to call the newspaper and put in an ad.

"Cal didn't want to do it. He got so upset he was almost hysterical. Finally, I was able to make him see that discounting everything was the only way we could raise enough money to keep the store open. Then people would buy.

"The sale was a tremendous success, but Cal was

afraid to try it again. He was worried that the manufacturers would stop selling to him. I had to convince him that the bottom line for appliance manufacturers was the number of units they sold. They didn't care what price he sold their washing machines for as long as he got rid of them.

"Today he tells anyone who will listen how *he* got the idea to start the first discount appliance store. He's concocted a story he's told so many times that he actually believes it!"

I'd heard Cal tell the story more times than I wanted to remember. "I had no idea that the whole concept for the business was yours," I said, shocked. "Why did you let him take all the credit?"

"Cal didn't have any self-confidence," she said, as if what she had done were the most logical thing in the world.

I looked at her, flabbergasted.

"I went to see Neil Hamilton this morning. I would have preferred going to a stranger, someone who doesn't know us in case things get ugly, but Neil is the best divorce lawyer in town. Cal called him while I was there."

"Did you tell Cal that you were going to go to Neil?"

"No," she said. "Cal wanted Neil to represent him. I got there first."

"Good," I said. "You scored the first point."

She sighed. "Oh, Ginger, this isn't about winning points. No matter how it comes out, I'm going to lose. Cal and I have been married for twenty-eight years. I don't have a career. I built my life around my marriage. Now I'm going to have to start all over again. One of my biggest fears has always been growing old alone, like my mother did. I'm not young, I'm not pretty. When it's finally over, I'll have some money, but then if a man shows an interest in me I'll wonder if his real interest is in my bank account."

"What if the man has more money than you do?" I said, thinking of Avery Laird.

"You're in incurable optimist," she said, smiling for the first time.

"I happened to meet someone today who does," I said. "I'll find out if he's married."

"Who?"

I briefly told her about my meeting with Avery Laird. "What a wonderful opportunity," she said. "I'm so happy for you."

Jane hadn't touched her tea. "Can I get you something else?" I asked. "Maybe ginger ale would help settle your stomach."

"No, thanks," she said. "If I'm going to be sick, I want to be sick in my own home." A sob caught in her throat. "I had hoped we would play with our grandchildren in that house. Now..."

She couldn't finish. She blew her nose, then rummaged in her purse for her keys. "Please stay for dinner," I said. "You don't have to eat if you don't want to. Just stay for the company."

"Another time," she said. My concern for her must have shown on my face. "You're such a good cook that it would be foolish for me to stay when I don't have an appetite. I'll take a rain check and use it when I'm hungry."

On school nights during the football season we usually eat at seven, but that night Buddy didn't get home until seven forty-five. I had made boneless chicken breasts in a wine sauce. By the time he arrived I had nursed the chicken, rice, and vegetable for so long, trying to keep it all warm and palatable, that I was no longer interested in eating. "Sorry I'm late," he said.

"It would have helped if you had called."

"I couldn't," he said. "I just spent the past hour and a half with Greg Shanley. Until this year he was the best inside linebacker the school ever had, a really talented kid. A field leader, too. Now he isn't playing worth a damn. The whole defense has fallen apart as a result. I know he's on drugs, I just know it! But I can't prove it. More important, I can't reach him."

For once it wasn't difficult to get Buddy's mind off the football team. "Your defense isn't all that's falling apart. Jane was here this afternoon. Cal wants a divorce. He's found himself a twenty-three year old to play with."

"Jesus, what a jerk!" Buddy said. "That's like trading a Mercedes for a Volkswagen Rabbit. Jane's a great lady. She's too good for him, and he's never had the sense to know it. How is she doing?"

"Not well."

While we ate, I told him about Jane's visit. Buddy was glad she had gotten to Neil Hamilton first. Before I had a chance to say that I had talked to Neil as well, Buddy started talking about the Shanley boy again, and the drug problem he suspected.

Buddy has always brought home the problems of his players and his teams, but that night I wanted to talk about my meeting with Avery Laird. I wanted Buddy to remember that I'd had the meeting.

He didn't. He went from the Thackers' divorce to the Shanley boy and the Clinton High defense like a traveler so intent upon reaching his destination that he doesn't even glance at any of the sights along the way.

At first, I was hurt. As I rinsed the dishes and put them in the dishwasher, I wondered if I were being unreasonable in expecting Buddy to ask about something that was so important to me. Then I wondered if my news about the Thackers had diverted his attention. I decided that it hadn't. By the time I finished wiping the counters and scouring the sink, I was angry.

I went directly upstairs and curled up in bed with a novel. I knew Buddy was in the family room watching a football game. Every Monday night he falls asleep during halftime. He always teased that it was my job to wake him up so he could go to bed and get a decent sleep. That night I turned the bedroom light off at ten fifteen. I don't know what time it was when he finally got into bed.

In the morning, he had a stiff neck. "I slept half the night in the chair," he said. "I guess you forgot to wake me up."

"I went up early," I said.

I don't know what made him finally ask. Perhaps he was remembering the previous morning. "How did your meeting go yesterday?" he said as he was getting up from the table.

"He's agreed to do the interview."

Buddy grinned. "That's terrific! Congratulations!" He started to bend down to kiss me and stopped, wincing. "Damn," he said, rubbing his neck.

VI

Neil Hamilton had the Letter of Agreement ready Wednesday afternoon as he had promised. It was a simple, one-page document that required three signatures: mine, Avery Laird's, and a witness.

We talked briefly about Jane. I brought up the subject because I wanted Neil to know how shattered she is. "She hasn't been able to keep food down since Sunday," I said.

"That's not unusual," Neil said. "A divorce is as traumatic as a death. In a sense it is a death, the severing of the deepest commitment adults can make to each other. Some people vomit, some get ulcers or go into deep depressions. Scientific studies have shown that divorce can precipitate serious illnesses; people's emotions affect their immune systems."

I shuddered. "How can I help her?"

"Just do what I imagine you've been doing: be a sympathetic listener."

I had noticed a box of tissues on Neil's wide mahogany desk, but until that moment I didn't relate the tissues to his work. "With all the divorces you handle, you must feel like you're presiding over ruins every day. Does it ever get to you?"

"Sometimes," he admitted. "I hate to see couples use their children as weapons: withholding visitation, poisoning a child against the other parent, even kidnapping. Warring parents don't realize how defenseless their children are, or how deeply they can be scarred.

"Most of the time, however, I'm just a negotiator trying to work things out."

"So that everyone is satisfied?"

Neil chuckled. "Only in the rarest divorces is anyone really satisfied. Most divorces demand compromise to get to a negotiated peace. In other words, both sides have to give."

"Make Cal give plenty for what he's done to Jane."

"I'll do the best that I can for her," Neil said.

I stopped to see Jane on the way home. She looked even worse than she did on Monday. Her color was still dreadful, and she had developed deep circles under her eyes. I remembered what Neil said about the immune system and became concerned for her. "I want you to eat dinner with us tonight," I said. "I insist."

"Thank you, but I can't. Cal will be here in an hour or two. He's been in Syracuse the past few days, probably staying with that Lianne. He's refusing to move out. Can you imagine: I'm going to have to live with him!"

"Why don't you move out?"

"And let him have this house to entertain his slut in?" she said. "Never!"

"Then what will you do?"

"I'll stay here."

"But that will be horrible. Think of the effect it will have on you. You'll end up with an ulcer, or worse. Please reconsider," I said.

"I had a locksmith come this morning. Now there is a deadbolt on our bedroom door. Cal can't get in unless he literally breaks the door down. I moved all of his things into one of the other bedrooms."

I tried again to persuade her to come to dinner, but she refused. "I have no appetite," she said, "none at all."

After I got home, I called Avery Laird; he wasn't in. I left my name and he called me later. I told him the Letter of Agreement was ready. "I won't be free until late Friday afternoon," he said. "Is five thirty too inconvenient?"

The time wasn't a problem. Buddy wouldn't be home for dinner that night; he had a football game in Camden. "Will someone be there to act as a witness?"

"I'll make sure of it," he said.

At dinner Buddy started talking about the Shanley boy again before I had a chance to talk to him about Jane. I was tired of hearing about Greg Shanley. "Can't we talk about something else?" I said. "Greg Shanley had been at our dinner table every night this week."

"He's in trouble," Buddy said, as though that was more than sufficient justification.

"I know," I said, "but he has parents. He's their responsibility, not yours."

"His parents are divorced. He lived with his mother until she remarried, but he couldn't get along with his stepfather so he moved in with his father. But his father travels a lot; sometimes he's gone all week.

I haven't been able to get in touch with him. Meanwhile, the kid is living alone, which is one of the reasons he got into trouble in the first place."

"You've done all that you can. Now you're just torturing yourself."

"There's the team to consider," Buddy said. "I pulled Shanley today and tried to work the defense without him, but they couldn't get it together."

"Give them a chance. They need time."

"They don't have time. They have a game Friday night, and if they play like they're playing now, they're going to lose."

"So they'll lose," I said. "It isn't the end of the world."

Buddy smiled wryly. "Maybe it isn't the exact end, but it's close."

"I know," I said, sighing. "Now can we talk about something else?"

I sighed because Buddy and I have gone over the subject of winning so many times that we know each other's arguments by heart. Buddy feels each one of his team's losses as his loss as well. He says it's his responsibility to help the kids on his teams play the absolute best that they can. I argue that even if they are playing their best, the kids on another team may be more talented. Buddy says that's where the coaching comes in: the best coaches can pull their teams to victory on any given night no matter how much talent there is on the other team. I argue that a win like that is a fluke.

Although I have never said it to Buddy, I believe that the coaches are playing each other through the kids, trying to prove that they are better. Of one thing

I am certain: Buddy doesn't like to lose. Ever.

We talked about Jane. I told Buddy how worried I was about her. "It isn't even a week," he said. "She has a lot of adjusting to do." Then he gave me one of his long, serious looks. "Don't get too involved or you'll end up going through her whole divorce with her."

"She's my best friend. I just can't walk away."

"I didn't mean that you should walk away. Call her, go out with her, but don't get into the thick of it with her. She's got a lawyer for that."

"How can you be so uncaring?" I said, shocked. "You've always liked Jane."

"I think she's terrific," he said. "You know that. But I don't like Cal, I never did. I've always felt he could be a really nasty piece of work."

"Remember how we used to wonder what it was that she saw in him? We could never figure it out."

"Maybe he's good in bed."

"Cal?" I said, laughing. "Never!"

"How do you know?" Buddy said, his eyes glinting with curiosity. "What has Jane told you?"

"She hasn't said anything. Cal Thacker is the most insensitive man I've ever met. I've never, not once, seen him think of anyone but himself."

Buddy was quieter than usual all evening, but I don't think his mind was completely occupied with football. What I said about Cal must have made an impression on him. Later we made love for the first time in nearly a week. Our sex life has always been good, if somewhat erratic, but after twenty-seven years of marriage I didn't expect any surprises. That night I was surprised. Buddy was amazing, really amazing.

The lawyer who kept me on the line so skillfully when I first got the option witnessed our signatures on the Letter of Agreement. He didn't look at all like I had imagined him. Squat, rumpled, and balding, he rushed into the office fifteen minutes late. "Sorry I held you up," he said, extending his hand. "I'm Bob Harken. I spoke with you on the phone."

"I apologize for being so curt," I said, remembering that I had hung up on him.

"Forget it," he said. "You accomplished what you set out to do."

We chatted for a few minutes after the Agreement was signed, then Bob Harken excused himself. "Bob told me you wouldn't budge, and he was right," Avery said after he left.

"He managed to keep me on the phone much longer than I wanted to be there."

"Bob is a great talker. He was that way even in college."

"Did you go to school together?"

Avery nodded. "Syracuse," he said. Then he smiled. "I was going to save that bit of information for the interview, which we should set up. How much time will you need?"

I wasn't sure. "At least two hours," I said, hoping it would be enough.

"Then I'll allow a little more," he said to my relief. "I have an appointment on Tuesday afternoon that I can re-schedule. Is Tuesday from two thirty until five or whenever we finish agreeable?"

"It's fine," I said.

We were the last people to leave the building. On our way out, he apologized for the late hour. "I hope I haven't interfered with any plans you have."

"I don't have any plans. The football team is playing in Camden."

Only later, much later, did I realize that he might have known the team was playing in Camden because he reads the sports section.

"Will you join me for dinner? We can talk about the interview."

I hesitated. It was one thing to go out to lunch with him to discuss a business deal and quite another to go out to dinner on a Friday night when my husband was out of town for the evening. "Don't be concerned about the propriety of it," he said. "We'll be in a public place. I'd like to try that new French restaurant, Henri's. I've been hearing positive things about it. If you see people you know, you can explain that you're interviewing me."

"I don't want people to know I'm interviewing you until I place the article."

"Then you can tell them that it's a business dinner, which it is."

It still didn't seem right. I was about to refuse when he added, "It doesn't make sense for each of us to eat alone when we could enjoy each other's company." He smiled. His teeth gleamed as white as his shirt in the semi-darkness. The air was quite cool, and neither one of us was wearing a coat. I couldn't take forever to make up my mind. With some misgivings, I agreed to go.

We drove in separate cars and met at the

restaurant, which is in a refurbished house in town. I'd been wanting to eat at Henri's since it had opened several months before but didn't suggest it to Buddy because it is so expensive. Even if we could have afforded to spend over one hundred dollars for dinner, Buddy would have balked. He says he can't enjoy a meal that costs a dollar a mouthful. I was wearing a red sweater and black wool slacks, an outfit that was too casual for Henri's and certainly not one that I would pick for business. But even if I was dressed properly and it was my only opportunity to have dinner at Henri's, by the time I arrived I was really uneasy about eating there with Avery Laird.

Although Henri's was elegant and the lobster bisque was superb, I didn't relax until the main course. My salmon was too good not to enjoy.

Avery was aware of my uneasiness. I think it might have amused him. "Are you always so conscious of everyone who walks into a restaurant?" he said when I looked at two couples being seated across the room.

"Yes," I said, "when it's after seven on a Friday night and I'm having dinner in an expensive restaurant with a man while my husband is working."

"You're working, too."

"I wouldn't call this salmon work," I said.

"How long have you been married?"

"Twenty-seven years."

"Impressive," he said.

He told me that he had been married twice, the first time to a girl he met in college. "We have a son. He came down with encephalitis after a vaccination when he was an infant. The encephalitis left him severely retarded. Everyone told us to put him in an institution, but my wife wouldn't do it. I think she truly believed that with love and care she could bring his mind back. He became her primary focus in life."

"Did she succeed?"

"More than anyone thought possible. She was able to get him toilet trained, even to ride a two-wheel bicycle. But his IQ never got higher than forty-six. When he was eighteen, she couldn't handle him any more. He had a violent temper, would get into terrible rages. He had to be placed in an institution."

I thought of Steve and Zack and felt grateful.

"We were divorced when he was five. Her personality had changed a result of all that had happened. A year later I got married again," he said. "It was a mistake."

His expression became serious. "What I've just told you is off the record. I would appreciate it if you don't ask personal questions when you interview me. I like my privacy. I've made every effort to protect it. I don't think the public has a right to know how many times I've been married or other details of my personal life.

"Maybe I'm more sensitive to it than most people, but it seems to me that a lot of what passes for journalism today is nothing but gossip."

For a moment I didn't know what to say. The Letter of Agreement stipulated a full interview but said nothing about content other than that his full cooperation was expected. "I appreciate your desire for privacy; however, I would like to write about you as a three-dimensional human being, not simply a business machine."

He looked startled. "Is that how you see me, as a *business machine*?"

"You've maintained your privacy so successfully that the public knows practically nothing about you. That's quite an accomplishment considering that the population of the entire county is under one hundred fifty thousand. People call you 'the man with the Midas touch.'"

"So I've heard," he said, "but that isn't what I've asked you."

The Blackhursts and the Lesters, couples Buddy and I have known for years, stopped at our table on their way to theirs before I could reply. I introduced them to Avery and explained that we were having a business dinner. Edith Blackhurst, a small, bony woman who has a quick mouth, looked at me suspiciously. "I thought you got out of real estate."

"I did," I said. "Now I'm just working on one property."

Fortunately, the maître-d' cleared his throat; he had other people to seat. The Blackhursts and the Lesters went to their table, supplied with something to talk about.

I told Buddy about my dinner with Avery Laird and meeting the Lesters and the Blackhursts, but I don't think he absorbed even half of what I said. He'd had a dreadful night. The team lost, and he caught Greg Shanley on drugs. When they arrived in Camden, Buddy noticed that Shanley got off the bus with his gym bag in one hand and all the stuff that should have been in the bag tucked under his other arm. Buddy made him open the bag. It was full of vomit. The boy had taken drugs before they left

Clinton Falls and had gotten sick on the bus.

A newspaper reporter called as we were getting ready for bed. Usually Buddy is patient with the press—as the coach of the football and baseball teams, he's accustomed to being interviewed—but that night he was short.

Neither one of us slept well. I rarely get indigestion, but something I had for dinner made me uncomfortable all night. Buddy was restless and wearily hauled himself out of bed to play tennis in the morning.

Zack surprised us by coming home for part of the weekend. He arrived in time for lunch on Saturday (Zack never misses a meal if he can help it) and explained that he wanted to finish his medical school applications where it was quiet. On Sunday morning I had breakfast with him while Buddy was playing tennis. I told him about the interview, and we discussed possible questions. At one point he pretended to be Avery Laird; he acted stuffy and difficult. I laughed harder than I'd laughed in a long time.

Before he left, Zack suggested that I buy a mini cassette recorder. "They're not expensive," he said, "and if you know everything is being recorded, you'll be able to relax."

It was an excellent idea. I bought one on Monday and saved the receipt, thinking that I could deduct it as a business expense if I sold the article.

Avery wasn't happy about the recorder. When I arrived, he welcomed me warmly. I noticed that an ice bucket, glasses, and drinks—hard and soft—had been set up on a cabinet that concealed a bar. But when I took the recorder out of my purse, he frowned. "I hope you don't mind my recording the interview," I said.

"I'm not comfortable with those things," he said, looking at the recorder as if it might catch him saying something he shouldn't.

I explained that I thought it would be to his advantage, that if I used any direct quotes I'd be able to get them exactly. "Besides," I said, "it should make it more like a conversation. I'll be taking notes, but they'll be brief."

Once the hurdle of the recorder was over, the interview went smoothly. At his suggestion we sat on the black leather chairs in front of his desk. I was wearing a turquoise sweater and gray wool slacks, which I had chosen in the hope that my casual clothes would set a relaxed tone. They may have contributed, although I doubt it. From his response to my first question until the end of the interview, Avery was cooperative, at times charming. I learned that he got into real estate in college. He bought his first property, a house that needed a lot of cosmetic work, with money he'd saved for his tuition. He took a semester off, painted and plastered, refinished floors, rebuilt the front steps and porch, and sold the house for such a nice profit that it financed the remainder of his education and gave him enough money to put a down payment on another house. "I was hooked," he said. "After that experience I knew I would spend my life in real estate."

He moved to Clinton Falls because he felt there was more opportunity here than there was in Syracuse. "Clinton Falls is nearly recession-proof because of the university and the hospitals," he said.

"I can't think of another place of comparable size that has a cancer research hospital as large and well-known as the DeWitt Clinton Cancer Center. There is also the Clinton University hospital, which draws people from all over the state. And then there are the laboratories and other businesses that the medical and educational complexes have spawned. Communities tied to education and medicine enjoy steady growth, which is heaven for a developer."

Off the record, he said, "Medicine is the sacred cow of American society. Costs keep spiraling, and although people complain, they pay without a fight. Last year I had a fractured arm. It was a hairline break, simple to set, but the total bill came to over fifteen hundred dollars. If I could set prices in real estate the way they do in medicine, I'd be a billionaire."

"You're not doing badly," I commented.

He laughed. "That's true, but I could be doing even better."

"How did you break your arm?"

His facial expression suddenly became closed. "An accident," he said in a tone that told me not to probe further.

I asked him about various projects he's done, from the Sunrise Mall to Saddleford. The only tense moments occurred when I questioned whether it was ethical for him to buy the block that included Geneva Stratton's property at depressed prices when he had inside information about the new bank building as a director of the Central New York Bank. His eyes turned a hard, icy green. "There was nothing either unethical or illegal about my buying the properties. It will not hurt any of the stockholders of the bank. On the contrary, they will benefit because the bank will benefit from the increased traffic that the mall will bring.

"Also, and I want to make a point of this: I did not start buying the properties until *after* the bank made a public announcement of its plan to construct the building," he said. "I hope that settles any concerns you might have."

Perhaps the memory of walking through Geneva Stratton's dusty store made me push on. I didn't want to antagonize him, but I couldn't let the matter drop. "The businesses on that block were all victims of competition from your Sunrise Mall. Does it ever bother you that those people suffered tremendous financial losses, some personal losses as well, as a result of your project?"

"Their businesses died as a result of their own inaction," he said, his voice turning as hard as his eyes. "No one forced them to stay there; they could have moved when their sales started falling off. They could have done what I'm doing now: they could have gotten together to build their own mall to compete with the Sunrise Mall."

"It's difficult for people to get together on a project of that size; there are so many different ideas and opinions."

He raised his hands, as if to halt further pursuit of the subject. "You can't hold me responsible for human nature. I'm a businessman. I look for opportunities, for projects that will be successful and give me a sense of satisfaction. If I hadn't built the Sunrise mall, someone else would have done it. It was inevitable that Clinton Falls would have a suburban mall."

He got up and went to the bar. "I could use a drink. How about you?"

"Nothing, thanks," I said.

He poured scotch over ice, then leaned against the bar. "Off the record," he said, "I'd appreciate it if you'd tell me why you pushed that line of questioning so hard. I thought this was going to be a friendly interview for a lightweight magazine. *Forum* isn't known for investigative reporting."

"Those questions are bound to be raised, especially after construction on the new mall begins. I wanted to ask them first. If you were in my position, you would have done the same."

He raised his glass, as if to toast me. "You're right," he said. "What are you going to put in your article?"

"I don't know, but you don't have to be concerned. I won't misquote you. It's all on tape, remember?"

"Yes," he said, glancing at the recorder. "As long as we're on this subject, I would like to make an observation that I hope you will include. The demise of downtown Clinton Falls was no different from the declines of downtowns in cities all over the country. It's been talked about and written about for years. People don't want to pay for parking when they shop or go out to eat. And they don't want to have to hunt for parking or be forced to park in areas that are inconvenient or worry about getting a ticket or having their cars towed away."

"How do you plan to accommodate parking for

your new mall?"

"I have several ideas," he said, "but they'll have to be worked out with the city. Without the cooperation of the city council, I'll be forced to abandon the project. I have no intention of building a white elephant."

During the last half hour of the interview, I learned that he is a football fan, that he breaks up the long Clinton Falls winters with vacations in the Caribbean, and that he frequently travels to New York City, where he visits art galleries and sees the latest Broadway plays.

Not bad, I thought, not bad.

At five fifteen, I rose to leave. My legs were stiff, the muscles in my neck tight. After more than two hours of intense concentration, I felt like a diver who had been poised at the edge of a board for ages, finally getting a signal to leap. I extended my hand. "Thank you," I said.

He held my hand in both of his. "I never thought I'd say this, but I enjoyed being interviewed," he said, adding, "at least most of it. Before I forget, do you have a copy of the option? Bob Harken will need it to prepare an assignment."

I gave him a copy, which he tossed on his desk. Then he walked me to the front entrance of the building. Rather than step around me, he leaned forward to open the door. For a moment his body was so close to mine that I could smell his aftershave lotion, subtle and expensive. At the time I thought nothing of it. I automatically stepped forward, saying, "Excuse me."

"Please call me when you've finished the article,"

he said.

The next day I went to see Geneva Stratton. She smiled broadly when I told her that I'd gotten a successful interview. "Did you give him the option?" she said, her excitement making her look years younger.

"Not yet," I said, explaining that an assignment had to be prepared first.

"That will give me time to get a phone. It'll make it easier for him to get in touch with me."

"I hope everything works out for you," I said.

"Oh, it will," she assured me. "The hardest part is over. There were times when I wondered how long I could hang on. And to think that I wouldn't have talked to you if it weren't for your name!"

"My name?"

"Middleton," she said. "The name Middleton is as good as any in Clinton Falls. Your husband is the coach, isn't he?"

"Yes," I said.

"My husband knew his father; they went to school together. John Middleton's pharmacy was something."

So was John Middleton, I thought. I asked her where she was planning to move.

"I was considering buying a two-family house if the rent I'd get on the second unit would cover the mortgage payments. Maybe you could show me some," she said, adding sharply, "but only if they're in good shape."

"Thanks," I said, "but as I told you, I'm not in real estate anymore."

"Too bad," she said. "You're good at it. If you do

as well in your new career, you'll be a success."

VII

It took three weeks to finish the article. I re-wrote it four times, letting it sit for a few days between each revision so I could approach it again with a fresh perspective. When I wasn't writing, I spent hours in the library reading interview articles in back issues of magazines. At some point it occurred to me that my reading was an education, as good or better than any journalism course I had ever taken. From each article I learned a lesson that I could apply to my own work.

On a rainy Saturday afternoon after I'd been working on the article for several weeks, Buddy asked if it was done. He'd been itchy all day. His tennis game had been washed out, and it was too wet for yard work. He'd had nothing to do except correct papers (he teaches geometry and trig), which didn't take long. Buddy is a whiz at math, and after so many years of correcting students' papers, his eyes move down a page catching mistakes as if they're signaling him with flags. When I told him the article wasn't finished, he asked what was taking so long. "It needs more polishing," I said.

"Maybe you're doing too much polishing. Let me read it."

"Since when are you an expert?"

He shot me a sly grin. "Since I have nothing to read and I don't feel like going out in this lousy weather."

On a Wednesday when I felt I had done all I could, I called my mother and asked what her plans were for the day. "I have a bridge game this afternoon," she said.

"The article is finished," I said. "I'd like you to read it. Could you come over this morning? You can tell me what you think at lunch."

"I'm on a diet," she said.

"I'll make you a salad," I said, pushing because I wanted her to read the article first. She is the most discerning reader I know. She was a librarian and has always read with a critical eye.

My mother arrived at eleven, dressed in a smart burgundy silk blouse and a burgundy-and-gray tweed skirt. The burgundy gave her skin a rosy glow and complimented her white hair and clear gray eyes. Although she has always dressed nicely, I've noticed that she dresses better now than she did when my father was alive. I have a theory about this: since his death she is only in the company of women, who notice what she wears; my father never did.

She read the article in the family room while I fixed julienne salads. When she was finished, she came into the kitchen. I didn't have to ask what she thought; she was beaming. "It flows like a dream," she said. "You did a splendid job. Tell me, is Avery Laird actually as interesting as he is in your article?"

I thought for a moment. "He's interesting, but he did have the benefit of editing."

She smiled. "We could all use the benefit of some editing."

During lunch she mentioned Jane and Cal. "It seems like everyone is talking about them. The other day Violet Bridgeport, whom I hardly know, started talking to me in the supermarket about the Thackers. I had all I could do to be polite. Afterward I remembered that you went to school with Violet's daughter. Do you ever see her?"

"Not if I can avoid it," I said. "Leslie is as big a gossip as her mother. She's been married twice, so she's been through the gossip mill as well."

"Thank goodness I don't worry about your marriage anymore."

"My marriage?" I said, astonished. "When did you ever worry about my marriage?"

"Years ago," she said. "You and Buddy were so fixated on each other from the time you first met. I worried that such a strong attraction would burn itself out. There was also the period you spent in Raleigh and Buddy's decision to leave professional baseball. I was afraid he would have regrets later. I remember how much you hated that place; you were miserable there. Funny, I don't recall ever hearing you or Buddy talk about that time."

"We don't."

My mother is a smart woman. Although her eyebrows rose in surprise, she didn't mention Raleigh or baseball again.

I had been so absorbed in the Laird article that I wasn't aware of how much talk was going on about Jane and Cal until Saturday night, when Buddy and I went to the Calloways' Halloween party. The

Calloways have had a Halloween party for the past fifteen years, maybe more. Each year I complained about having to dream up characters and costumes, but we always had a good time. This year was different: I had no trouble deciding on who we would be, but I didn't have a good time.

I went to the party as Guinevere, wearing a reddish-blond wig and a long gown with an empire waist that I found in a vintage clothing store. Buddy, wearing a purple robe and carrying Excalibur, went as King Arthur. From the time we arrived until we left, it seemed that one person or another was talking about the Thackers. At first, I was put off. Then I was irritated. Finally, I was angry. "Almost everyone there was at Jane's housewarming," I said as we drove home. "They're all supposed to be her friends, and they were entertaining themselves at her expense. They have no loyalty!"

"Loyalty isn't as much fun as gossip," Buddy said. "Besides, Cal got the brunt of it. I didn't hear anyone say anything unkind about Jane. They feel sorry for her."

"I know," I said. "That's what bothers me most."

"Why?"

"I would shrivel up if I knew people felt sorry for me. Jane would, too."

"Then we'll have to stay married."

"So people won't feel sorry for me? Thanks," I said. "You're making me feel like a charity case."

Buddy reached over and put his hand on my thigh. "Believe me, sweetheart, you'll never be a charity case."

Although I'd sent the article and a cover letter to

Cordell Wylie at *Forum* on Friday, Buddy didn't read the final draft until Sunday evening. He'd been too busy and too tired, and definitely out of sorts. The football team had lost every game since Greg Shanley had been dropped. Each loss cut Buddy to the bone. He worked the boys and himself as hard as he could. "The defense almost has it together," he kept saying, as if he were trying to convince himself. "We're going to end the season winning."

Three more weeks of football, I thought, waiting for him to finish reading. It had been a rough season. Maybe this year I could finally persuade him to stop coaching football and just coach baseball. But I'd have to do it fast. Once they had a win...

Buddy put the article down and gave me a home-run grin. "It's great," he said. "I'll drop it in the mail for you tomorrow morning."

"I already mailed it. That's a copy."

"Oh," he said.

No one but me could have caught the hurt in his voice, a barely detectable drop in tone. "I was anxious to get it out of the house."

"Laird comes off quite well."

"He asked me to call him when the article was done."

"Why?"

"I'll find out tomorrow," I said. "Now I want to talk to you about football."

Buddy groaned. "The answer is no."

"Give me a chance. You don't know what I'm going to say."

"Yes, I do," he said. "You're going to tell me how tired I look and how draining coaching is, and then you're going to ask me to drop football."

"Why don't you?" I said. "Why can't this be the last season? The boys are gone; I'm out of real estate. September and October are such lovely months. Why can't we enjoy them together?"

"I'll think about it."

"No, you won't," I said.

On Monday I called Avery. "I have a business proposition I'd like to make to you," he said. "Are you free for lunch on Thursday?"

"If it's a business proposition, I can come to your office."

"You could," he said, "but a good lunch might make you more receptive. I'll meet you at Treehaven at twelve thirty, if that's all right."

"It's fine," I said.

With the article finished, I was again restless and bored. It seemed worse this time because I had spent nearly a month doing something I had really enjoyed. I didn't want to start another article until I heard from Cordell Wylie, so when Thursday arrived, I was more than ready to meet Avery.

He was taking off his coat when I walked into Treehaven. It was a Burberry trench coat, which probably cost more than Buddy earns in a week. "Perfect timing," Avery said, smiling warmly.

"I thought I was a few minutes early."

"We both are," he said.

Again, we were seated at a window, but the sky was overcast, a dismal gray that made the leafless trees rimming the golf course look dark and uncompromising. "I hoped you'd bring a copy of the article," he said after we ordered, "but I guess you didn't."

"Is that really why you invited me to lunch?"

"No," he said. "I asked you here because I want to offer you a job. I know you're interested in writing, which I respect. You'll be able to work out your schedule so you can allow for that. Occasionally you might have a full week, but it shouldn't happen often."

"Then it's a part-time job?"

"Between twenty and thirty hours a week," he said. "You'll make offers on properties, look for potential projects, evaluate proposed projects, and so on. I want your input, as well as your skill in closing deals."

"Don't you already have people to do those things?"

"There has been some reorganization. Several people were asked to resign."

"Why me?"

"You're enterprising," he said. "You know what to look for and you have good instincts. The last time we ate here I got more valuable input from you on a property I was considering than I did from my people. In the end, I avoided what could have been an expensive mistake."

What he said was flattering, but I couldn't completely believe him. "There are a lot of people in Clinton Falls who have far more experience than I do. Also, my experience is in residential real estate."

"Years of experience are just quantity," he said. "I'm looking for good instincts and creativity: either you have them or you don't."

"What makes you think I'm creative?"

He laughed. "You accomplished the impossible: you got me to agree to an interview."

It sounded good, but I was still suspicious. Maybe it was too good. I picked at my pasta primavera, wondering what to say. "How is your lunch?" he asked.

"Good," I said. Actually, the vegetables were overcooked.

"Your starting salary will be sixty thousand," he said, "with occasional bonuses."

My mind stopped at sixty thousand. It wasn't that far away from what Buddy earned. I put my fork down and looked at him, incredulous. "You'll be replacing people whose combined salaries were considerably higher," he said in response to my amazement. "I'm careful with my money. If I weren't, I wouldn't be in the position that I'm in today. As far as I'm concerned, if you accept the job I'll be getting a bargain."

I folded my napkin and placed it on the table. "It's a wonderful offer," I said, "but I'd like to think about it. Can I let you know on Monday?"

"I'll look forward to your call," he said.

On our way out of the dining room he stopped briefly at several tables. At each table he said, "I want to introduce you to Ginger Middleton. I'm hoping she'll join Laird Enterprises." He said this as if I were a prize he hoped he'd win. It was flattering and embarrassing at the same time. The two men at one of the tables recognized the name Middleton. They knew Buddy and spoke glowingly of him. I was accustomed to strangers speaking glowingly of Buddy, but Avery wasn't. I glanced at him, concerned that he might be irritated, and was surprised to see that he looked pleased.

Avery helped me with my coat and walked me to my car. There was a quality to his attentiveness that I hadn't noticed before, something I couldn't name. It was enormously flattering. Later, much later, I realized that I was responding to more than his job offer. But that day I was unaware of his intentions. He wanted me to work for him; he valued my ideas and my judgment, and he was offering me a salary that was beyond anything I would have dared to ask for a part-time job. It was incredible, which is exactly what Buddy said that night after I told him about the offer.

"Sixty thousand for a part-time job!" Buddy said, looking at me skeptically. "That's incredible! There has to be a hook somewhere."

"There isn't," I assured him. "Think of what it will mean: we'll be able to help Zack, maybe take some trips, go out to dinner more often..."

"Then you've already decided."

"How can I refuse? It's an amazing offer."

"That's what bothers me," Buddy said. "It's too amazing. Avery Laird is known for driving a hard deal. He wants his money's worth, and then some."

"I'm supposed to be replacing several people."

Buddy cocked his head to one side and studied me. "Do you believe that?"

"I don't think he'd lie to me."

"What about your writing career?"

"One article that hasn't been accepted isn't a career," I said. "I'll have time for it."

Buddy still wasn't satisfied. All weekend he poked and probed, raising issues like my writing career that I knew really didn't matter to him. When he started again on Sunday after he came home from a meeting with the football team, I had finally had enough. "What's really bothering you?" I said.

"I don't know. I just can't put my finger on it, but my instincts tell me that you shouldn't take the job."

"Well, my instincts tell me that I should," I countered. "I'm forty-eight years old. I spent most of my adult life taking care of my husband and children. Driving car pools and doing laundry aren't skills that shine on a resume. The one career I had, selling real estate, I hated. This may be the only job offer I'll ever get. I can't refuse. It's like a miracle."

"That's what bothers me," Buddy said. "My instincts tell me there's no such thing as miracles."

We didn't discuss the job again. I had to get busy in the kitchen because Jane was coming for dinner. It was the first time she accepted my invitation since she and Cal had broken up.

Jane looked remarkably well. She'd had her hair re-styled and was wearing a stunning black and white sweater I hadn't seen before. At first I thought her new hair-do and clothes were responsible for the improvement in her appearance; however, during dinner I learned that the real tonic was what she was about to do to Cal.

"Cal has been claiming that business has been off for months so he can force me to take a smaller settlement," she said. "At first I believed him. I was so dazed and heartsick I would have believed anything. But one day he pulled into the driveway, and I saw her in the car. He didn't bring her in; he isn't that stupid. But just seeing her in *my* driveway made me so angry that I stopped feeling sorry for myself and decided to fight back.

"I was so busy with the construction of the house that I hadn't paid much attention to the business. I had always kept an eye on things, particularly the advertising. It occurred to me that I hadn't seen as much advertising as usual during the summer, which is the busiest season in the appliance business. A weak summer can kill a year. I decided to investigate and discovered that he had done half the amount of advertising he had done the year before. Half!" she said, her color higher than I had ever seen it.

"Then I went back, month by month, checking the advertising and the sales figures. I checked at every location, making sure I wouldn't be there when he was. By the time he caught on, I had all the evidence I needed. Neil and I are going to court tomorrow morning to have a receiver appointed to operate and manage the business. Cal will no longer be running *Cal's*!"

While I was marveling at the restorative powers of revenge, Buddy was asking questions. "I don't want to be a pessimist, but sometimes thinking you have a sure win is as close as you come to getting one. What if the judge doesn't grant your request? Shouldn't you prepare yourself, just in case?"

Jane smiled. "Thanks for your concern," she said. "Normally I'd be worried, but Neil says the evidence we have is as clear as anything we could have wished for."

"Who will run the stores?" Buddy asked.

"One of the general managers will, temporarily. I own fifty percent of the stock, and I intend to watch everything that's going on."

"What will Cal do?" I said.

"I don't know, and I really don't care. We also think we'll be granted an order that will force him to leave the house."

Buddy and I looked at each other. We were both thinking the same thing: Cal could be a mean piece of work. "Be careful," I said. "If you're successful tomorrow, you'll be forcing Cal to leave the two places that are most important to him—his business and his home. He could try to get even."

"He could, but he won't."

"How can you be sure?" Buddy said.

"Cal is all bluster. There's nothing behind it. Also, my attorney is better than his, and he knows it. Cal backs away from a fight unless he thinks he can win, and tomorrow he's going to find out just how badly he can lose."

Suddenly tears glittered in the corners of her eyes. "All those years of marriage, and now it's as though there were never any happy times, nothing but two lawyers battling over money and property in court."

I had made chocolate mousse for dessert. Buddy attacked his with gusto, but Jane picked at hers, her appetite gone.

"Jane is going to be fine," Buddy said after she left. "Cal is the one who is going to be the big loser. I guess there is still some justice in the world."

"It isn't over until it's over," I said.

Buddy frowned. "What's that supposed to mean?"

"It will take Jane years to recover from this, if she ever does," I said. "While she was helping with the dishes, she told me she was afraid of becoming a bitter old lady."

I didn't tell Buddy that Jane also said, "You and Buddy have the best marriage of all the couples I know. I can't imagine anything ever coming between you."

At the time it didn't seem worth mentioning.

VIII

I started working for Avery the day after I called to tell him I would accept the job. The weeks flew between that first Tuesday and Thanksgiving. Most of my time was spent becoming familiar with the considerable number of projects Laird Enterprises is involved in, far more than I expected: office and medical buildings, a suburban shopping plaza anchored by what will be the largest supermarket in Clinton Falls, a high-tech industrial park, two residential developments, and the proposed downtown mall. With the exception of the residential developments, the name *Laird Enterprises* doesn't appear in association with any of the projects; instead, the names of dummy corporations owned by Laird are on all of the signs and letterheads. One day I asked Avery why he hid behind dummy corporations. "I wouldn't put it quite that way," he said. His voice had a distinct edge. "Seeing the name *Laird* plastered all over town might antagonize some people. I don't want to incur resentment. The fact that Laird Enterprises owns the corporations isn't hidden: it's a matter of public record, and it's always reported in the paper."

"If they see it at all, most people see it only once

and probably forget it," I said.

He smiled at me as if I were a star pupil.

The office I was given, which was as stark and modern as the rest of the building, was on the same floor as Avery's; Bob Harken's office was down the hall. Several times a week Bob stepped into my office to chat for a few minutes. Although his manner was casual and friendly, my instincts told me that his interest was serious: he was taking my measure, evaluating me for what I believed were his own purposes. I much preferred the open curiosity of Avery's secretary, Gloria Evans, who invited me to join her for lunch toward the end of my first week.

We went to a restaurant near the mall. It didn't take long to tell Gloria what I sensed she wanted to know about me: that I was happily married and not interested in anyone's job but my own. I encouraged her to talk and learned that she came from a poor family and had a bad early marriage; she raised her only child from that marriage, a daughter, alone. She has worked for Avery for years, since he first came to Clinton Falls from Syracuse. "You're probably wondering if Avery and I ever had anything going," she said with her characteristic candor. "The answer is *no*. I kind of hoped something would happen after my marriage broke up. I must have been sending out signals, because one day Avery sat me down and told me that as attractive as I was—I don't mean to brag, but I was a knockout when I was younger—he would never let our relationship extend beyond the office in case things didn't work out. He told me I was the best secretary he ever had, and he knew he could never get another one as good. At the time, I didn't know if it was a polite brush-off or if he really meant it."

She spread her manicured fingers, displaying the flashy rings she wore. "He's shared his success with me, so I know he really meant it."

It was from Gloria that I learned I was replacing two young law school graduates. "I guess Avery thought that he and Bob could train them, but neither one had time," she said. "Those two kids didn't know anything about anything, just a lot of dry stuff they learned in school that was useless."

Gloria also told me that my getting the interview from Avery impressed the staff more than anything that had happened around Laird Enterprises in years. "I wasn't surprised when Avery hired you," she said. "Since you did the impossible once, I expect he thinks you can do it again."

When I moaned, she said, "Well, you can always fall back on your writing."

Perhaps her remark was prophetic, for when I got home I found a letter from Cordell Wylie accepting my article. *Forum* would pay one thousand dollars upon publication in January.

Buddy wanted to take me out to dinner to celebrate, but I had stopped and bought swordfish steaks on the way home, so we opened a bottle of good wine instead. "To your success," Buddy said, raising his glass. "And to me, for being the smartest guy on the block."

"What makes you so smart?" I said, feeling like the other half of a comedy team.

"I married you and got a woman of many talents."

"Thanks," I said, "but whether or not I have talent

remains to be seen. The subject sold that article, and I know it."

"Your next article will prove it. Call Wylie and get a few suggestions on topics from him."

"I'll call after the holidays."

"Why wait? You've got his attention now."

"I also have a new job, and I have Thanksgiving and Christmas to prepare for," I said. "At the moment, I have a full plate."

"Well, mine's empty," he said, spearing the remaining piece of swordfish. "Sensational dinner, sweetheart. If you can develop into as good a writer as you are a cook, you'll have a fabulous career."

I didn't say anything. At the time I felt his remark was patronizing, even though I understood why he could have made it. He was still uneasy about my working for Avery. Whenever he asked about my job there was a note of suspicion in his voice, as if he were searching for some hidden agenda. "It's insulting," I said one night. "You're constantly looking for devious reasons as to why Avery hired me. What you're really saying is that I'm not worth what I'm being paid."

"Do you think you are?"

"Not yet," I said, "but I'm new on the job. Eventually I hope to be."

"Expensive training period," Buddy said, as if that were yet another reason to be suspicious.

I worked only two full days the week of Thanksgiving. I explained to Avery that both of my sons were bringing friends home for the holiday. "I really won't need you until the following Monday," he said. "We have a meeting with the mayor at ten o'clock."

I noticed that his expression changed when I told him about Steve and Zack bringing their friends home. He looked almost wistful, as though he would have liked to be included. For a moment I hesitated, wondering whether I should invite him to Thanksgiving dinner, and just as quickly decided against it for several reasons, Buddy not being the least of them. He probably had plans with friends or family anyway.

Having a full table and a full house added to my enjoyment of the holiday. As a child I was uncomfortable on Thanksgiving because my parents and I went to other people's houses; dinner was rarely at our house because there were only three of us. I didn't like being a guest and used to envy my friends their larger families and full tables. Every year I would secretly wish that someday I would celebrate Thanksgiving at a full table in my own home. Sitting with the boys and their friends, Buddy, and my mother and her sister, I remembered that secret wish and felt especially grateful.

I had invited Jane and her daughters, but they didn't want to be in Clinton Falls for the holiday, for which I couldn't blame them. Jane won her battle in court; however, she paid a terrible price for it. The day Cal left the house he punched her in the face; not only did he crack two of her front teeth, but he tried to rape her as well. Fortunately, the rape failed because he couldn't get an erection. Hysterical, she called Neil Hamilton, who called the police. Cal was arrested and charged with assault and battery and attempted rape. His lawyer offered much better terms for the divorce as a bribe to get Jane to drop the charges. If the case went to trial, it would get enormous publicity, and Cal's reputation would be ruined. Jane decided to let him squirm until the last minute. "I want him to have a good dose of suffering," she said. "While he was enjoying himself with his girlfriend, I was so paralyzed with shock and hurt I could barely function. Even now I have to force myself to get out of bed in the morning. The only thing that's kept me going is fighting back, which is hurting me as much as it is him, maybe more.

"He told someone that I'm going to drop the charges. 'Jane couldn't take that kind of publicity,' he said." She smiled, a bitter smile. "He's right, of course. But I'm not going to drop the charges until the day of the trial. Then he will know what it's like not to want to get out of bed in the morning."

Jane was in my thoughts all Thanksgiving day. I imagined her eating in some cold Manhattan restaurant with her daughters and could have wept for her. As we were getting ready for bed, Buddy told me that he thought it was the best Thanksgiving we'd ever had. "You did a great job," he said. "You've got that meal down to perfection."

My eyes misted. "It's not the food that matters, Buddy. It's having our family—the boys and their friends, my mother and aunt—all together."

He put his arms around me. "You're right, sweetheart. You're absolutely right."

I had been too busy all weekend to wonder why Avery wanted me to attend his meeting with the mayor, Ernie Boldt. On Monday morning we drove downtown in Avery's Mercedes; the rich smell of leather mingled with the subtle scent of Avery's aftershave lotion in the heated car. I expected him to brief me, but instead he asked if I had a pleasant Thanksgiving and talked about a winter storm that had been forecast to arrive late in the afternoon. Finally, when we were a few blocks away from city hall, I said, "I don't know what you expect of me at this meeting. I don't feel prepared."

"Just follow my lead and you'll be fine," he said. "By the way, how well do you know the mayor?"

"I've met him a number of times, but I really don't know him. He was a classmate of Buddy's."

Avery nodded. "What does your husband think of him?

I hesitated. "Not much."

"Any particular reason?"

"Buddy might have told me, but at the moment I can't recall."

I knew why Buddy didn't like Ernie Boldt, but I felt I'd already said more than I should. Buddy has no use for Ernie because he thinks Ernie is a despicable coward. When they were kids, there was an unspoken agreement that no boy would ever take another boy's bicycle without his permission. One day Ernie disappeared with another boy's bicycle. Later, when he spotted the boy coming after him, he gave the bike to his younger brother to ride. Not only did he blame his brother for taking the bike, but he stood and watched while the boy beat his brother into a bloody mess.

Buddy told that story and other Ernie Boldt tales to Steve and Zack as they were growing up. Ernie became such a successful negative example in our house that the worst insult our boys could shout at each other when they fought was the name *Ernie Boldt.*

Ernie Boldt's office was as ornate as his manners. He was effusively cordial, welcoming us and seeing to our comfort like an overanxious butler. When he started to rattle on about Buddy, as if he and Buddy were the best of friends, Avery cut him off by saying, "Ginger told me that you and her husband were classmates."

Ernie may be a coward, but he isn't stupid. He got the drift and shut up. Then Avery took control of the meeting. He told Ernie that he held title to all the land he needed to build a new downtown mall and that an architect was finishing the plans, but he would not consider breaking ground until he had a commitment from the city to build a new parking ramp on the block behind the mall, which was vacant. "The city can't afford that big a project," Ernie said, his pale skin growing paler. "We're in deep water now."

"The city can't afford not to do it," Avery responded coolly. "Before I hired Ginger, she interviewed me for *Forum* magazine. I was very candid in the interview, which will be published in January. To put it simply, I said I would be forced to scrap the project without a guarantee of substantial new parking."

Ernie, ever the politician, gulped and turned his milky eyes on me. "I didn't know you were a writer. How did you get an interview with Avery? From what I've always understood, that's next to impossible."

"I was instrumental in getting the last piece of property he needed for the mall."

"Good work!" he said, as if I'd done it for him. "I'm sure you appreciate how important that mall is to my plan for a downtown renaissance."

Avery smiled at me encouragingly. "Yes," I said. "I also appreciate the enormity of the investment it will take. The amount of risk is too great without a guarantee that new parking will be created."

The meeting ended with Ernie protesting that there was enough parking, but he would present the matter to the city council. "Typical politician," Avery remarked with disgust as soon as we were out of earshot. "One foot on each side of the fence."

On our way back to the office, Avery told me that I had handled the meeting very well. "I only spoke once," I said.

"You said the right thing at the right time."

Maybe I did, but I couldn't shake the feeling that despite the salary he was paying me, I had been used.

Although I didn't intend it, my uneasiness might have showed. Avery doesn't miss anything. He is as sensitive to subtle changes in people's behavior as Buddy is to the slightest change in the spin of a ball. A few days after our meeting with Ernie Boldt, Avery called me into his office. "I want you to look at these," he said, handing me a roll of papers he withdrew from a tube.

The papers included a full survey and several drawings of sections of the Leverton farm, which is, without question, the finest property in the county, over five hundred acres of rolling land that has a small lake and several streams. The house—a mansion, really—is gray stone; it has hand-carved woodwork in fine woods, marble floors, and intricate plaster ceilings and moldings that can't be duplicated today. "Is it for sale?" I asked.

"I want to be up front with you," he said, making sure we had eye contact. "I've tried to approach Nell Leverton three times in the past three years to make an offer on the property, and she won't even meet with me."

"Then she isn't interested in selling."

Avery's eyes narrowed. "I'm not so sure. Rumor has it that she's been quietly selling all the livestock. I understand even Oliver Leverton's prize bulls are going to be shipped for auction. At the club I heard that her daughter is coming for Christmas."

"So you think this would be a good time to make an offer, and you want me to approach her."

"Exactly," he said.

"What are your plans for the property?"

"I want to develop a substantial portion of it—at least half—in stages. It will be upscale and restricted: lots of three acres or more, a minimum square footage per house, all exteriors in brick or stone, and an architectural review board, which I should have had with Saddleford, and so on. It will be the most exclusive address in the county."

"What do you plan to do with the house and the barns?"

"I'm going to live in the house," he said. "I really haven't thought about the barns."

I tried not to look surprised. "The house is magnificent, but it's huge."

He smiled. "If I get insomnia, I'll have plenty of rooms to walk around in."

I realized that I didn't know where he lived. I

didn't ask when I interviewed him, because I knew how strongly he felt about his privacy. Curious, I asked.

"I have an apartment at the Rexford. It's convenient, and all the hotel services are available."

The Rexford is the nicest hotel in town. All the medical VIP's who come to Clinton Falls stay there. "Why would you give up a hassle-free existence for the headaches of maintaining a house?"

My reaction seemed to surprise him. "It's just recently that I decided to keep the house for myself if I bought the property. Maybe I hope the eventual benefits will more than outweigh any headaches."

"I'd like to make copies of these and get back to you," I said, rolling up the papers.

"I don't want to pressure you, but timing could be important here."

"Don't be concerned about Darcie Leverton. Unless she's changed radically, she never gave a fig about the farm. It's Nell Leverton you have to worry about."

Again, he seemed surprised. "You know the Levertons?"

"Darcie and I are the same age. We went to each other's sweet-sixteen parties."

I could have added that Darcie Leverton had a crush on Buddy and threw herself at him every chance she got, but so did a lot of other girls. It was long ago, a bit of irrelevant history.

For the rest of the week I pored over the surveys, drawing and redrawing lines and making notes. I also drove out to the Leverton property. The road had been plowed after the storm but was still slick in spots.

Covered with snow, the gently-rolling land was gorgeous, a mixture of open pasture and thickly-forested slope. As I drove back I thought about the Levertons. Oliver Leverton was the Horatio Alger of Clinton Falls, the fourth or fifth son of a poor farmer. Through hard work and an advantageous marriage (his wife's family had money), he eventually became the president of the Central New York Bank. Oliver learned banking; a feeling for land and livestock was in his blood. He bought the best land in the county as soon as he was able and then stocked it with prime cattle, which he selectively bred. Vials of semen from his bulls sold for incredible sums. For a while when I was a teenager there was a rash of semen jokes about the Leverton's bulls. I can still remember the boys' guffaws.

If they had been my father's bulls, I would have tried to disappear for at least five years. Darcie Leverton, however, encouraged the jokes. She was a plain, nearsighted blond who had inherited neither her mother's looks nor her father's brains. Maybe she thought the bulls would give her an aura of sexiness. All she had, though, was a fast reputation. Unfortunately for Darcie, her older brother, Peter, got all the hereditary gifts. He was fast also, but in a different way. Peter Leverton raced cars, motorcycles, boats, anything that moved. He was killed in a car crash his last year in college.

Before I met Buddy I had a crush on Peter Leverton. I felt bad when he died.

When I finally met with Avery on Friday morning, I spread a survey I had marked on his desk. The Leverton property is rounded like the cap of a mushroom, with the straightest, widest portion fronted by a state-maintained road. I divided the mushroom into three uneven sections; the largest section, which included the house and most of the lake, was on the far right. "I know you were planning on dividing the land differently," I said, "but I'd like you to hear me out."

Avery leaned back in his chair, his eyes drifting back and forth between me and the survey, while I explained why I felt the largest section should remain intact and undeveloped. "From what I remember, the talk around town was that Nell Leverton was the driving force behind the grand house, not Oliver. His tastes were a lot simpler. He's been dead for nearly six years, a long time for her to continue living alone in that huge place, with the additional responsibility of employing enough people to take care of the cattle and the land, unless she was deeply attached to it. My mother says Nell is at least eighty."

"So you think she would be more receptive to an offer if you showed her this proposed division," he said.

"Not proposed," I said. "Guaranteed."

Avery sat up. "What do you mean, *guaranteed*?"

"The purchase offer will have a deed restriction barring that section from subdivision."

"There's no way I'll agree to that! When I buy land, any restrictions placed on it are there to suit *me*, not the seller!"

I expected a strong reaction, but not that strong. His jaw was set, his expression hard, his eyes a brittle green. "Then, in my opinion, there's a fair chance you won't be buying the property."

"I'll go as high as six million, though I want to try to keep it at around five."

"I don't think this is about money," I said. "Nell Leverton has plenty of money and no one to leave it to but a daughter. There are no grandchildren." I paused, then plunged on. "She's an old woman. Her daughter is married to a career diplomat and moves from one remote country to another. All Nell Leverton has left as a reminder of a marriage and a life that was full and happy is her home. She'll be a lot more willing to part with it at a reasonable price if she has some guarantees."

Avery looked at me intently. "Tell me what you have in mind for the other two sections."

"I think you should subdivide the smallest section first, make each parcel a minimum of five acres instead of three. You should get at least twenty lots, probably more, depending on the division. You could price them at three-hundred-fifty-thousand to five-hundred-thousand each."

"That's a little steep."

"Plots that are five acres or better could be marketed as mini-estates, which will set the development above all the others in the county. There is nothing available now that comes close, and there are plenty of people in Clinton Falls who want to move up. They would pay that and more; they're sitting on their money now, waiting for the housing market to improve."

"It's irresistible," he said, raising his hands in a gesture of surrender. "I'm sold."

Nell Leverton was easier to sell than Avery. When I showed her the proposed division of the land

and told her that the section on which the house stood would be protected in the deed, I could actually see her relief. Her entire body seemed to relax. She had always been slender, but age and reduced her to bones and pale, blue-veined skin. Even her eyelashes had disappeared; her hairless lids were rimmed in pink like a white rabbit's. I remembered how formidable she had been and how uncomfortable she'd always made me feel. Both Nell and Darcie were snobs. Nell hadn't changed. As she was ushering me into her antique-filled living room, which was about forty feet by twenty-five feet, close in square footage to a small house, she made a comment about it being a pity that I had to work. I stifled a surge of anger and managed to tell her sweetly that working was my choice and I enjoyed it.

Negotiating the price went more smoothly that I had anticipated. My first offer was for four million. "My land is worth considerably more than that," Nell said, sniffing to let me know how deeply she'd been insulted.

"I won't disagree with you," I said. "The issue here is not so much what the land is worth as it is finding qualified buyers. There aren't many people in Clinton Falls who are in the market for a property of this size, with all the maintenance this house and land requires, which would be a major factor in trying to sell it. I don't know of any farmers who can make you that generous an offer, and I'm sure you want the house and land kept as they are now."

I reminded her of the deed restriction and the lack of qualified buyers every time I upped the offer. It wasn't long before she agreed to sell for four million, three-hundred-fifty thousand. The land was worth far more than that. The comment Nell made about it being a pity that I had to work made me change my starting offer. Instead of offering four-and-a-quarter million as I had planned, I cut the opening offer by two-hundred-fifty thousand dollars, wondering if I could make her pay for her remark. Oh, did she pay! I would have felt guilty if I hadn't recalled stories about Oliver Leverton's sharp negotiations for the very same land, in which he was rumored to have pressed an unfair advantage.

Avery wasn't in, so I told Bob Harken. "Two for two," he said, looking amazed. When I told him the price, he said, "Wow!"

I hadn't realized how badly Buddy's suspicions about my job had eroded my self-confidence. For the first time in weeks I felt really capable again, as if I could accomplish almost anything.

That night I took Buddy out to dinner to celebrate. We went to his favorite Italian restaurant. I was so excited I couldn't stop talking. "Avery would have gone as high as six million. I saved him one million, six-hundred-fifty thousand dollars! Now will you believe I'm worth the salary he's paying me?"

Buddy smiled. "I never argue with a lady when she's paying for dinner."

Bob Harken prepared a Contract of Sale, which Avery and I took to the Leverton place late in the afternoon a week before Christmas. "Quite an entrance, isn't it," Avery remarked as we drove up the long, tree-lined road to the house.

"Quite," I said, looking at the huge trees, stark against the bleak winter sky.

Nell Leverton's attorney, George Cunningham, read the Contract of Sale before Nell signed it. He looked as old as Nell, an ancient gentleman who had tremors in his head and hands. His mind, however, was sharp. He read the contract quickly, requested a few minor changes that Avery agreed to, and then presided over the signing and initialing.

Nell poured glasses of sherry. "To the new owner," she said, her pink-rimed eyes resting on Avery. "I hope you will come to love this place as much as I do."

He gave her a charming smile. "I'm sure I will," he said.

She was so taken with Avery that she talked to him exclusively, as though George and I weren't in the room. She would have kept him for hours, refilling his glass with sherry, if I hadn't gotten up to leave. Nell blinked, as though she'd forgotten I was there. "Darcie will be arriving on Monday," she said. "Do call."

I said I would, although we both knew I wouldn't.

It was dark when Avery and I left. He paused to gaze at the house after he opened the car door for me. I could see the excitement in his face, the warm flush of his skin despite the cold. "Congratulations," I said.

He turned to me. "I should be congratulating you."

Quickly, almost rudely, I got into the car. Somehow I knew that if I didn't he would have kissed me. It would have been a kiss of shared victory, a kiss of triumph, but I couldn't let it happen.

When he got into the car, I saw that all the excitement was gone from his face. I had destroyed a wonderful moment for him and felt awful. "Let's celebrate," I said impulsively. "I'll cook a victory dinner."

"How can you do it? It's five thirty."

The same way I do it every night, I thought. "Magic," I said.

We went the office first. While Avery talked briefly to Bob about the changes in the Leverton contract, I called Buddy to tell him that I was bringing Avery home for dinner. I asked him to put a bottle of wine in the refrigerator and to pick up any newspapers and magazines that were scattered around. The house was straightened when I left in the morning, but Buddy has a tendency to turn every room he's in into a den.

I drove my car, Avery following in his, to the supermarket. He looked lost as we went from aisle to aisle. I was taken aback when he tried to pay at the check-out counter. "You're a guest," I said.

Buddy was waiting for us. He hadn't changed and was wearing olive corduroy slacks and a sweater he had put on in the morning. One of the benefits of being a teacher, he says, is that he doesn't have to suffer the tortures of a shirt and tie. I didn't want him to suffer, but I couldn't help thinking when I introduced him to Avery, who was wearing a custom-made suit, that it would have been nice if he had at least made the effort to put on a pair of wool slacks. If Buddy had known what I was thinking, he would have said, "That's your problem." And he would have been right.

I put out cheese and crackers, and Buddy made drinks. The two men sat in the living room and talked about sports while I cooked. Dinner was ready in half an hour. It was easy to prepare, cut-up boneless chicken browned in olive oil and then simmered with chopped tomatoes, wine, basil and mushrooms, served over fettuccine. A salad with oil-and-vinegar dressing and a warm baguette rounded the meal.

We ate in the dining room. A silk flower arrangement I had used for years as an impromptu centerpiece showed its age when I took it out of the china cupboard, so I polished some apples and arranged them in a rustic basket which I placed on the white tablecloth. The apples glowed a deep luscious red in the candlelight.

Conversation seemed to flow easily. There were no uncomfortable moments until Avery complimented me on the dinner, which he was eating with obvious enjoyment. "It's nothing," Buddy said. "Ginger does it all the time. She's a great cook."

"You're very lucky," Avery said.

"It was a safe bet. Her mother is a great cook, so I figured she would be, too."

There was smugness in the tone of Buddy's voice that made me inwardly wince. Embarrassed, I quickly changed the subject.

We were talking about the downtown parking problem when I brought in the dessert, which was simple to make and looked spectacular. I put a slice of pound cake topped with a scoop of pineapple sorbet in three oversize wine goblets and then spooned raspberry sauce over the sorbet. "First the Leverton property and now this," Avery said, looking at me as I set the goblet before him. "You are a woman of many talents."

"Yeah," Buddy said, "for a while I wondered why you hired her, what your intentions were."

For a moment there was a silence so total the air was completely still. Buddy's spoon was poised over his goblet, but his eyes didn't leave Avery's face. "My intentions?" Avery said with a wry smile. "I intend to marry your wife."

"Sure," Buddy laughed. "Sure."

After Avery left, Buddy helped me clear the table and do the dishes. While I was washing the pots, I said, "I've been thinking of fixing Avery up with Jane."

"She's not his type."

"How would you know what his type is?"

"That's easy," Buddy said. "Didn't you hear him? You're his type. He said he's going to marry you."

"Sure," I said, laughing.

IX

On the first Monday of the new year, our telephone rang at about nine thirty. Buddy answered, and when I heard him say, "Hoot? I'll be damned!" I shut the book I was reading and closed my eyes.

"You'll never guess who that was," Buddy said when he came back into the family room.

"Hoot," I said, "and you invited him for dinner."

Buddy grinned self-consciously. "I guess I talk kind of loud when I get excited. Poor Hoot has lung cancer. He was told it's inoperable; he's here for a second opinion."

"It's amazing he was able to find you after so many years."

"He remembered that I came from a small town in Central New York that has a big cancer hospital. With the internet, the rest was easy."

"What time is he coming over?"

"Around five." Then Buddy frowned. "Damn, I have a meeting that could run over. But you should be home. You can explain if I'm late."

Not only had Buddy volunteered to have me cook dinner, but he also expected me to entertain Hoot until he arrived. I had enjoyed the Christmas holiday, but it meant a lot of extras: extra cooking, extra cleaning, extra laundry. The house was hopping, the boys and their friends coming and going at all hours. Buddy loved all the traffic. I did, too, but I was glad when it was quiet again. "Let's take Hoot out to dinner," I said.

Buddy looked at me as though I'd said something mean. "Hoot's alone here, and he's dying. The least we can do is give him a home-cooked meal."

The royal *we*, I thought, *we* meaning Ginger.

Before Hoot called, I was tired. After Hoot called, I was tired and irritated. Time hadn't changed anything: I was still reacting badly to Hoot.

Hoot, whose real name is Henry Hooter, was Buddy's closest friend when Buddy played baseball for the Raleigh Caps. During the first spring and summer of our marriage, Buddy spent as much time with Hoot as he did with me. The Raleigh Caps played five night games a week and a game on Sunday. When they weren't playing, Hoot, Buddy and I were often a threesome. Hoot was, as he put it, "between women," so he hung out with us.

I was miserable in Raleigh. I couldn't adjust to the heat and the humidity. When the air didn't sizzle, it steamed. We lived in a rooming house that had no air conditioning. Some days were so humid I couldn't dry off when I got out of the shower.

My problem wasn't just with the climate or the rooming house, a seedy place owned by a widow whose name was Mrs. Moneypenny. If ever a name fit, Mrs. Moneypenny's did: she was the most tightfisted person I've ever known. Even her face was pinched and narrow. On the rare occasions when she smiled, her lips barely stretched across her teeth. At Mrs. Moneypenny's the towels were worn so thin you could almost see through them and the light bulbs weren't much brighter than candles. The food she served was unforgivable.

I knew when I married Buddy that he would play ball, but I never imagined my life would be like it was in Raleigh, the long nights and longer days, the tired small-town stadiums, the shabby rooming house and the heat, the ever-present heat. I felt as though I had gotten married and gone straight to hell. No bride ever loved her husband more than I loved Buddy. I was crazy about him, hungry for him all the time when we were in Clinton Falls, but not in Raleigh. It was too hot. We never made love during the day, only late at night when the temperature in our room dropped to the low eighties.

Although I didn't recognize it then, I suffered most from loneliness. I had never been away from Clinton Falls before, away from my parents and friends. I had nothing in common with the other baseball wives and girl friends, who spent their time experimenting with make-up and hairstyles and studying the latest fashion magazines. Most came from either farms or small towns in the South and Midwest; none of them had been to college. My speech, my clothes, my education made me different from them, and they reminded me of it often. They weren't intentionally unkind. Rather, they simply couldn't relate to me, or I to them. They only reason we were all there was because our men were playing baseball.

Buddy got along well with the fellows on the

team. Men judge each other on a different basis than do women; they look beyond the superficial. The fellows might have warmed to Buddy because of his easy way with people and his fabulous grin, but what really mattered to them was that Buddy is a tough competitor and a team player. More important than their friendship, he had their respect. The fellows were all polite and friendly to me because I was his wife. I was polite and friendly back, but I couldn't relate to them much better than I could to their women. The only thing we had in common was Buddy.

Besides Hoot, Buddy was friendliest with a fellow who was considerably older than us. Sal Capizzi was from Pennsylvania. He had bounced from farm team to farm team for over ten years, never making it to the majors. Sal was a big, good-looking fellow; he had curly black hair and smooth olive skin darkened to a rich color by the sun. At first I thought Sal was single. Every time I saw him he had a pretty girl on his arm. Southern women went crazy over Sal. They literally draped themselves over him, using their arms and bodies like nets as if attempting to capture this man who was so exotic to them. Their behavior made me wonder if he were the only Italian male in Raleigh, if not in all of North Carolina.

One Sunday Sal went out for a late breakfast with Buddy and me. After we ordered, Sal left the table to make a telephone call. His breakfast was starting to get cold when he came back. "Sorry," he said, sliding into the booth. "I had to get myself out of hot water. I was supposed to call my wife yesterday and forgot."

I quickly looked down at my plate, hoping he didn't see the shock I knew was on my face. Later I learned that he and his wife had three little girls. Off-season he supported them by working in a pizzeria he owned with his brother.

I tried to find out as much as I could about Sal. I asked Hoot and some of the other players. They all said pretty much the same thing: Sal was a good, solid player who should have made it to the majors. When I asked why he didn't, they shrugged and talked about luck and timing and then gazed off, as if the answer were somewhere in the distance. I sensed that they were gazing off not so much in response to my question as for themselves, hoping they might see something that would prevent them from ending up like Sal Capizzi, a solid player stuck forever in the minors.

I liked Sal and enjoyed his company. He was easy to be with. But he terrified me.

Buddy saw Sal as a mentor, a supportive, experienced friend who gave him good advice. I saw Sal as an object lesson: he was what Buddy could become in a dozen years—a cheating husband, an absentee father, a man struggling to reach a goal that each year was becoming more impossible to attain.

When I asked the fellows about Sal, I tried to act as though I was just passing the time and fooled everyone but Hoot. After he told me what I had already learned from the others, he said, "You think Buddy'll end up like Sal."

"No," I replied too quickly.

Hoot looked at me shrewdly. He was taller than Buddy, and beefier—broad shoulders, big arms and chest. His nose, which was long and flared at the nostrils, veered to one side; it must have been broken once. "Buddy'll make it. His chance will come. It's a matter of timing. It's all a matter of timing."

"Timing is just another way of saying luck. Sal hasn't been lucky; other guys, even good players, haven't been, either."

"Buddy's got real talent. He can play ball," Hoot drawled. "Don't you worry about him. He'll make it."

It was in mid-season when Hoot and I had that conversation. Scouts had been showing up at the games, and a fellow whose name I can't recall had just been picked for the Triple A team that owned the Class B Raleigh Caps. Buddy had been injured the year before, so this was his first full season. He was giving it all he had, going for extra practice and playing his best in every game. And he was playing well, but for some reason he wasn't picked. Maybe he hadn't been playing long enough to prove himself. We knew most fellows weren't picked their first season; however, Buddy had been so outstanding throughout high school and college that we might have subconsciously thought he would be chosen, though we never actually discussed it. Then one night when a scout was in the stands, Buddy's batting was off. It happened again the following night. For a week or so, until Buddy figured out what was wrong, we went through separate hells. I worried that it was my fault, that I was affecting him badly I remember forcing myself to smile until my face hurt, as if smiling and showing a positive attitude might solve the problem. Buddy didn't say anything. He had grown quieter, more introspective, at times brooding, not at all like the Buddy I had loved since I was sixteen. Even after he solved the problem and was batting well again, he still brooded, but only with me. He didn't show that side to his teammates.

Toward the end of the season we started to bicker. I became frightened, thinking I was to blame because I hadn't adjusted well, because I wasn't a perfect baseball bride. "Everything I do seems to be wrong," I said late one evening after a particularly bitter argument, trying to stifle my sobs so they wouldn't carry through the thin walls. "Maybe I should fly home."

He looked as if he agreed. "It's up to you," he said.

We had argued because I had waited up for him. It was during the week; the team had a night game out of town. He'd told me that he planned to come back to the rooming house after the bus dropped the team off, but instead he went out drinking. He walked into our bedroom at three in the morning, reeking of beer. I had been reading in bed, but when I smelled him from across the room I closed the book and turned off the light, too upset to say anything. He tripped over something in the darkness, lost his balance and landed on the floor, cursing.

It was my fault. I had turned off the light. I had also waited up for him. "Like a jailer," he said.

Buddy slept after we fought, but I didn't. I cried until I couldn't cry anymore and tossed until about seven in the morning, when familiar cramps forced me out of bed. I got my period a week early.

I showered and dressed and went for a walk. At eight in the morning it was already sizzling; it was going to be another brutal day.

I don't remember where I walked or what I saw. I

had never felt so miserable or frightened or defeated in my life. When I came back to the rooming house, Mrs. Moneypenny was sitting on the front porch, rocking in an ancient wicker chair. She looked at me knowingly and suggested that I might be in a family way. I put my hand over my mouth to catch a sob and hurried inside. "Thought so," Mrs. Moneypenny said.

Buddy wasn't in our room. I took my suitcase out of the narrow closet and started to pack. Tears streamed down my cheeks as I removed my trousseau from the dresser drawers. When I picked up the lovely lingerie that my mother and I had shopped for, I cried so hard I became sick to my stomach and ran to the bathroom, dry heaving.

I was folding the last of my things when Buddy came into the room. "Ginger," he said, his voice strained and low, "please don't do this... just a few more weeks and it'll be over... it's the last season... I'm quitting."

That Buddy would play professional baseball had always been a given, an assumption never questioned, as immutable as gravity. "No," I said, panic rising in my throat, "you can't quit, you can't. You'll feel differently when I'm gone."

Buddy put his arms around me. "You're not going until you leave with me. We're walking out of here together, and we're never coming back or looking back."

And we never did. At the end of the season we returned to Clinton Falls and lived as though Raleigh had never happened.

Not talking about Raleigh was a huge mistake. I knew it when we were back in Clinton Falls, but I felt so guilty that I couldn't bring it up. I believed, I truly believed that if I had adjusted better in Raleigh, Buddy wouldn't have quit. I was afraid he would begin resenting me, if not hating me, because he gave up what someday could have been a glorious career. So I kept quiet, and he did, too. Later there were moments, like the time we were in the University of Michigan hospital after Steve's wrist was operated on, that I knew we were both thinking about Raleigh, but neither one of us uttered a word. Each year of silence I felt the weight of another layer of guilt. Buddy was such a talented athlete that I was absolutely certain he would have been a star in the major leagues if it weren't for me. I never questioned this, not once, until Hoot came for dinner.

Buddy wasn't home when Hoot arrived a few minutes after five. At first seeing him was a shock. The Hoot I remembered had a head full of sun-streaked hair and an unlined, ruddy complexion. The man at my door was pale and bald and had deep creases in his face. But his drawled greeting was pure Hoot, a warm hug accompanied by "Hey, good to see y'all."

After I took his coat, explaining that Buddy was detained at a meeting, we went into the living room. "Can I fix you a drink?" I asked.

"Bourbon, if you've got it."

"Water?"

Hoot shook his head, coughing.

While I made our drinks—my bourbon with water—I thought about why I had always reacted badly to Hoot. We were often a threesome in Raleigh, and when we were together I usually felt left out.

Hoot was a great talker; he would get Buddy talking about baseball and the two of them would go on for hours, as if I weren't there. It was almost impossible not to like Hoot: he had a warm, friendly personality, and he thought the world of Buddy. But it was also almost impossible for me not to resent him.

He was coughing again when I brought in a tray with the drinks and crackers and cheese. I gave him his drink. "Maybe this will help."

The coughs sounded shallow, like a reaction to dust or a mild allergy. Somehow he managed to sip the bourbon. "Whew," he said, looking white and drained when the attack finally subsided. "Sometimes nothing works. But let's change the subject. We got a lotta years to catch up on."

He told me he had been married twice and had a son, nearly grown, from his first marriage. "I have a great business–the best barbecue restaurant in all of Greensboro. Once I wanted my boy to step into it, but now I don't know, unless he can keep away from the hickory smoke. I figure it's the smoke that made me sick.

"It don't seem fair," he said. "It's just the past few years that the business got really solid. I was a long time in getting started, bounced around in the minors for a dozen years. Baseball cost me both my marriages, a home like y'all got here. I wish I would've been smart and quit like Buddy. He had the odds all figured out.

"I remember like it was yesterday when he told me he was quitting. We were on the bus coming home from a night game. We'd won, but Buddy was real down. I asked was something bothering him. That's when he told me. I thought he was crazy and told him so. 'Y'all got as good a chance as any guy on this bus of making it to the majors,' I said.

"I must've been a little too loud. A couple of fellas' heads turned. Buddy said we'd go for a beer when the bus pulled in."

Hoot coughed and immediately reached for his bourbon. "So we went for a beer," he continued when the coughing stopped. "Buddy said he'd been thinking about quitting for a while, but seeing Methuselah on the bench that night just about did it for him."

I was stunned by what he was telling me. "Methuselah," I managed to say. "Who was Methuselah?"

"Aw," Hoot said, "I can't remember his real name. He was on the team we played that night, a guy who'd hung around the minors for seventeen, eighteen years, maybe more. That's why they called him Methuselah: he'd been around forever. His hair was getting gray, what was left of it. I never forgot what Buddy said: *he said he didn't want to get old on the bench.*

"We talked and drank and drank and talked. We sure did get loaded." Hoot smiled at the memory. "At the time I thought I had failed because I couldn't turn Buddy around. He had real talent, as good an eye as anyone I'd ever seen. Now I know my failure was not taking what he was saying to heart. If I had, my life would have been different, a lot different."

I heard the garage door opening. "Buddy's here," I said. "He's really been looking forward to seeing you."

"I can't say I'm happy about what brought me

here, but I'm sure glad I came. Seeing Buddy will take the edge off the day. It's been a rough one."

It sure has, I thought, my head reeling from what he had told me.

I didn't trust myself to talk to Buddy about what I had learned from Hoot until the following evening, and even then it was probably too soon. Zack says my temper is like a summer storm because my anger comes and goes quickly. But this time my anger was more like a hurricane: it swept in and it stayed, intense and unrelenting. Anger kept me up most of the night and made it nearly impossible to concentrate at work during the day. At dinner I hardly said a word; I was so upset I had difficulty swallowing and pushed my food around on the plate. Buddy didn't notice that my dinner was uneaten until I got up to take the dishes to the sink. He had talked throughout the meal about Hoot, who had been told by doctors at the DeWitt Clinton Cancer Center that his lung cancer was indeed inoperable. "You didn't eat," Buddy said, looking at my plate. "Are you feeling okay?"

"I'm upset," I said.

"I guess I shouldn't have gone on and on about Hoot."

"I feel sorry for Hoot, but he's not the reason I'm upset. Hoot and I had quite an enlightening conversation before you came home last night. Among other things, Hoot told me that you decided to leave baseball because you didn't want to get old on the bench. He also told me you made your decision the night you got drunk with him after a game."

Buddy shrugged. "It happened long ago. What difference does it make?"

"*What difference does it make?*" I repeated, wanting to scream, wanting to throw the dishes against the wall. "All these years you let me think I was to blame for your quitting baseball. Whenever anyone asked you about it, you always said your wife was unhappy, she would have left you."

"It's true: you were miserable and you were packing. But I always said it like a joke."

"It was no joke! I was packing because I thought you wanted me to leave. I thought I was hurting you rather than helping you. I begged you not to quit. I begged!"

"It's history, Ginger. Forget it."

"NO!" I said. "I want to know why you never told me you made the decision to quit before I started packing. I want to know why you never told me about Methuselah and growing old on the bench. I want to know why you let me believe all these years that you quit because of me."

"You were a factor."

"Not according to Hoot!"

"Forget about Hoot!" Buddy said. "Just drop it!"

I stormed out of the kitchen, tears of anger and frustration streaming down my face.

Buddy and I didn't speak for the rest of the evening. I stayed in our room, remembering all the times I'd felt responsible for Buddy quitting, the terrible guilt I'd carried the years we struggled financially while jerks like Cal Thacker made bushels full of money. The more I remembered, the angrier I became. I was not, as Buddy demanded, going to forget what Hoot told me. I wanted Buddy's acknowledgment. I wanted his apology.

Buddy doesn't apologize easily. It's difficult—almost impossible—for him to admit that he's wrong. He also insists upon having the last word in any disagreement, as though the final say tips the scale to his side. I've always thought his compulsion to have the last word was childish, in infuriating juvenile game. I was not going to play his game.

Over the years our fights had grown shorter. Instead of carrying on an argument as we once did, everything would be forgotten and forgiven, usually in a day, sometimes in an hour or so. But not this time. Two days later I was barely speaking to Buddy. I wouldn't let him win me over with a smile or a hug. When *Forum* arrived in the mail, I put it on the coffee table in the living room without saying a word about it. Although I should have been thrilled and excited when I opened the magazine to look at my article, I felt nothing other than a sense of satisfaction. A check for one thousand dollars came in a separate envelope which I decided to deposit in a small account I've had in my own name for years.

Buddy spends most of his time in the family room; he didn't notice the magazine, so when our friends started calling to congratulate me, he was taken by surprise. "Why didn't you tell me *Forum* came?" he said, looking wounded.

"Why didn't you tell me when you decided to quit baseball?"

"One has nothing to do with the other."

You're wrong, I thought, *you're wrong.* But rather than argue again, I walked away.

Avery was pleased with the article. He came into my office Friday morning waving a copy of *Forum*.

"You did a great job!" he said, beaming. "The article is balanced and fair, better than I probably deserve considering the trouble I gave you. Let's go out to lunch to celebrate."

"Thanks, maybe another time."

He put down the magazine and placed his hands on my desk, leaning toward me. Still tan from a holiday trip to the Caribbean, he looked dashing, the darkness of his skin accentuating his graying temples and deep green eyes. "Is something wrong, Ginger? You've been different this week, quieter."

"It's nothing, probably post-holiday blues."

"Maybe a change of scenery will help. I'm going to Niagara Falls next Thursday to look at a factory outlet mall. This morning I set up a meeting with the developer. I want you to come with me. We'll fly there early Thursday morning and be back in time for supper."

"Why an outlet mall? Where would you open it?"

"There's a property for sale east of Syracuse that has great access to the Thruway. The structure on it was built for light manufacturing and could easily be divided and converted into stores."

"What about parking?

Avery gave me an approving smile. "The property is close to six acres. Want to see it?"

"After we go to Niagara Falls."

When Thursday arrived I was more than ready to leave. Buddy and I were stepping around each other like courteous strangers; we were civil, but we didn't communicate more than was absolutely necessary. Even the weather seemed to reflect what was happening to us. It turned bitter cold over the weekend, with biting winds and chill factors of better than minus fifty degrees. On Saturday I met Jane for lunch. She told me that the lawyers had worked out most of the details of her divorce. "Neil says we should have a signed agreement in a week or so," she said. "He thinks I've done extremely well. In the end, Cal folded on nearly everything."

Jane didn't sound or look victorious, or even happy. As I listened I became chilled, though the restaurant was warm despite the frigid winds outside. I thought about Buddy and me and the days that had passed in which we'd hardly spoken, and I shivered. But driving home I thought about the guilt I had carried for twenty-seven years, twenty-seven years in which Buddy hadn't told me the truth about the biggest decision in our lives.

Nothing changed when I got home.

Avery and I took a plane to Niagara Falls early Thursday morning. I wore high leather boots and a warm long coat, which proved fortunate. Western New York was as cold as Clinton Falls, and we were told when we arrived that a severe winter storm was predicted.

The developer of the outlet mall sent a fellow named Ralph to meet us at the airport. Ralph, who had a beer belly and a full, pleasant face, took us out for breakfast and gave us a brief history of the mall before driving us there through an unattractive area that had a mix of every type of business from fast food to light manufacturing. "You probably want to look around on your own for a while," he said.

We set up a time and place to meet. Ralph reminded us about the storm warning. "I'll be back sooner to look for you if the weather turns bad," he said, glancing anxiously at the darkening sky.

Avery and I decided to look at a section of stores opening directly outside like a plaza before going into a large building that housed additional stores. "Most of the license plates on the cars are from Ontario," I said.

"Canadians come here to spend their money because they get more for it."

"How successful would this place be without them?" I wondered aloud.

"Hmmm," Avery said. "Interesting point."

The stores all had after-Christmas sales, but the merchandise was sad and picked over. "What do you think?" Avery asked as we started to walk to the main building.

"It might not be fair to judge because it's the end of the season," I said. "I recognized some of the merchandise: it's from last year, which is no bargain when you can get as good a discount on the latest styles at department store sales." I didn't add that I suspected some of the merchandise we were seeing was specifically manufactured for the stores, as it was in other outlet malls I had been to in the past.

We had been in the main building for about fifteen minutes when we heard our names called. It was Ralph. "Sorry, folks," he said, rushing up to up to us, "I have to cut your visit short. The storm is heading this way, and it's a bruiser. I've made reservations for you at a hotel. I'll wait while you buy yourselves whatever you need—we can stop at a drug store so you can get some toiletries–but I'd appreciate it if you'd move quickly. We don't have a lot of time."

Avery reached into his pocket and pulled out folded bills held by a silver money clip. "Here," he said, peeling off three fifties.

I didn't want to take money from him. "I'll use a credit card."

"Cash is quicker."

"He's right," Ralph said.

I ran to a lingerie store, where I literally pulled things off the racks: underpants, a nightgown, a robe in a rich shade of emerald green, and a pair of slippers. After I paid for the items I met Avery and Ralph, who were waiting for me. It was snowing heavily when we got outside.

While the men brushed off the front and rear windshields, I sat in the back seat wondering whether it was wise to go anywhere. I started thinking about colossal snow storms that had hit Clinton Falls, blizzards whose statistics exceeded Buffalo's famous Blizzard of '77, and decided to suggest that we stay where we were. "Don't worry," Ralph said confidently. "I've lived here all my life. I could get you there practically blindfolded."

Our stop at the drugstore took more time than we expected. I didn't buy much, just a toothbrush, toothpaste, deodorant, skin lotion, and a small bottle of aspirin, but we had to stand in line for close to ten minutes because there was only one checkout cashier. Avery held onto my arm we left the store. Fortunately, Ralph had kept the car running and the headlights on so we could find him in what had become a blur of white.

It wasn't long before we all felt blindfolded. Ralph kept wiping beads of perspiration off his forehead as the car crept through what felt like a wall of snow. All I could see was white, with the exception of occasional glimmers from street lights that were no brighter than dying candles. Every once in a while Avery turned to check on me; the worry creases between his eyes growing deeper. "How are you doing?" he kept asking.

"Fine," I answered each time, my voice and smile getting more and more strained. Not only was I apprehensive, but I also had a full bladder. We'd had breakfast hours ago, and I'd had a second cup of coffee.

Ralph had to stop the car a number of times because he could see absolutely nothing. The snow came down so hard and so heavily that the windshield wipers moved in smaller and smaller arcs, unable to clear it away fast enough; periodically the men had to get out of the car and brush the snow off to free the wipers again. And to add to the tension, Ralph had the car radio on so we sat like prisoners unable to escape disc jockeys spending their adrenalin on up-to-the-minute doomsday reports: with relish they interspersed lists of closings with grim descriptions of road and storm conditions. Those professional talkers had enough material to keep their mouths busy for hours; they were the stars of the storm, and they were clearly enjoying every moment.

After better than two hours of inching through that white hell, any doubts I ever had about the existence of miracles were dispelled when Ralph said,

"This is it."

I looked out the window and saw the faint shadow of a building. Ralph chuckled when we thanked him. "You folks will sure have a story to tell when you get home."

Avery put his arm around me and guided me into the hotel. The lobby was full of stranded travelers. My first thought was that our rooms had probably been taken. "Oh, no," I blurted.

"Don't worry," Avery said, "Ralph told me that he guaranteed our reservations."

The rooms we were assigned were on the same floor a few doors from each other. A harried fellow at the front desk handed us our keys and pointed in the direction of the elevators. Finally, I thought, I'll be able to use the bathroom.

"You probably want to freshen up," Avery said when we stepped out of the elevator. "Call me when you're ready and we'll get something to eat."

Once inside my room, I immediately turned on the light in the bathroom. I cursed when I saw that water was within a few inches of the top of the toilet bowl and slowly rising. I tried calling a service number, then the front desk, but no one answered, so I got back on the elevator and went downstairs, where I was directed to a public bathroom.

It was mid-afternoon before Avery and I were finished with lunch. The harried fellow at the front desk had been replaced by a pale young woman who told us that the commode in my room couldn't be fixed because the hotel repairman left when the storm started. "We had to turn the water off to the commode so it wouldn't flood the room below," she said. "I'm sorry, but we have no other rooms."

"We'll work it out," Avery said as we walked to the elevator.

I went to my room to call Buddy while Avery made calls in his room. The secretary at the high school rang Buddy's office, but he didn't answer so I left a message about the storm and the telephone number of the hotel. I turned off my cell phone to save the battery; the trials of the day caught up with me then. I felt drained. Avery's line was busy so I knocked on his door and told him that I was going to take a nap for a few hours.

I didn't sleep well. Perhaps it was expectation, but I kept dreaming that Buddy was calling, the phone was ringing, and then I'd wake to silence. Finally, I got up and washed my face and brushed my teeth. Buddy still hadn't called.

Avery and I stopped in the lounge after dinner. The dimly-lighted room was packed with people sharing their storm stories. They stood with drinks in their hands telling strangers tales of their trials in past storms, as well as this storm. There was a feeling of high spirits, of survivors bonding together as people bond when they've withstood the elements. At first Avery was aloof; he watched and listened as if he were witnessing a strange phenomenon. But soon he dropped his reserve and was talking and laughing like everyone else. We had such a good time that when the bartender announced the storm had passed over, there was a collective sigh of disappointment.

It was after eleven when Avery and I stepped into the elevator, still laughing at a story we'd heard. I'd had several drinks, and my head felt pleasantly fuzzy.

We decided that since I had a bathrobe and he didn't, I would sleep in my room and use his bathroom.

The message light on my telephone was blinking. I immediately called Buddy.

Our conversation was brief. He wanted to know where I had been all evening, he had called twice. After I explained, he didn't say anything. "Buddy," I said, "are you still there?"

"Yeah."

"It's stopped snowing. I should be home tomorrow."

"Fine," he said, as though it made no difference. Then he said good-by and hung up.

It wasn't fine. Buddy's voice was so cold it swept away the pleasant, fuzzy feeling I'd had. Suddenly the troubles of the day seemed minor. I was devastated.

I don't know how long I sat on the bed feeling as frightened and lost as I had in Raleigh years ago. It was as if nothing, yet everything, had changed.

When Avery knocked on the door, I was startled. He had taken off his suit jacket and tie, and had rolled up the cuffs of his blue shirt. "Are you all right?" he said.

Until that moment I had been dry-eyed, but at the tone of his voice, his genuine concern, my eyes filled with tears. And then his arms were around me and his mouth was on mine; it happened so swiftly it seemed inevitable. I forgot about Buddy and Raleigh, I forgot about everything. My head was filled with Avery saying, "I've wanted you for such a long, long time."

He took my hand and we went to his room, where we made love with such urgency that we were breathless when we finished. "Now," Avery said when he reached for me again, "we can take our time and enjoy each other." Then there was nothing but sensual pleasure, a steady rise of passion building to a need so powerful I cried out in a voice I didn't recognize when he entered me.

Gray light seeping in through the closed drapes woke me at dawn. For a moment I didn't know where I was. Then I remembered. I felt the warmth of Avery's naked body next to mine, the stirring of his morning erection. *Oh, God, Buddy*, I thought, sick over what I had done.

We were able to get a flight back to Clinton Falls late in the afternoon. I wanted to rent a car and leave in the morning, but road conditions were poor with blowing, drifting snow. I was so anxious to leave that I couldn't sit still: I walked the corridors in the hotel; I paced inside the room. "Please, Ginger," Avery said finally, holding me by the shoulders, "you have to stop this. I know you're upset. I understand. But you're only exhausting yourself. We have to talk, and we should talk now."

"Not now," I said, wanting only to move, "I can't think."

His grip on my shoulders tightened. "Then just listen: I'm in love with you; I have been for a long time. I want you to marry me."

"I'm already married."

"I know, but what has happened between us has to change that."

"No, it doesn't," I said. "What happened was a mistake, a terrible mistake." Avery flinched. "I'm sorry, I don't want to hurt you," I said. "You're very attractive and I responded to you, but what I did was wrong. Buddy and I have been married for twenty-seven years, and until last night I never betrayed him, not once. I feel sick about it, so awful I don't know how I can face him."

"Buddy can't give you what I can," Avery said, his eyes flashing, "and I'm not talking about what money can buy, although I won't minimize it. I want you with me on the beach in the winter, and in the theater in New York. Since the day Nell Leverton accepted our offer I've imagined living in the mansion with you. We can renovate the place together, get the best people to restore it to what it was. We can share our lives creating and building. We're a perfect team in every way."

"I'm sorry," I said, wanting to weep, "I'm truly sorry."

Before we left Avery insisted upon visiting the falls, which he had been told were the most breathtaking during the winter. I had seen the falls several times during the summer and wasn't interested in seeing them again, especially not in the state I was in, but when we got there I gasped at the sight. The scene was dazzling, a fairyland of ice and snow glittering in the winter sun. Everything was coated with ice–railings, trees, shrubs, benches. All the turmoil I was feeling was replaced by awe. Avery and I carefully walked to an observation area, where we watched the water thunder over the precipice and hit the rocks below, to rise again in the mist that iced everything around us. Avery took my gloved hand in his. "I'm glad we could see this," he said, his voice barely audible above the roar of the falls.

The expression on his face was different from any

I had seen before, tender yet sad; there was almost no trace of his sharpness, his steely determination. I squeezed his hand.

We said little on the trip back to Clinton Falls. Before we parted at the airport he bent his head, brushing his lips against my cheek. "I meant everything I said," he whispered.

Buddy's car was in the garage when I got home. I sat in the car after I turned off the ignition, afraid to face him. As I've explained, Buddy and I can read more in each other's expressions and gestures than some people can read in books.

I heard water running in the kitchen when I stepped into the foyer. "I'm home," I called, although I was sure he'd heard the garage door open.

If things had been right between us, he would have come to greet me with a kiss. Instead, I took off my coat and boots and went into the kitchen, where he was drying a small sauté pan. He had been working in the basement or on his car because he was wearing one of Steve's old Michigan sweatshirts and a pair of faded jeans that hugged his body. Buddy looks great in jeans; I ached when I saw him. "I didn't know when you'd be home, so I made myself a couple of eggs," he said. "Do you want me to scramble some for you?

"Sounds good," I said.

I really didn't want the eggs. What I wanted was to erase the past twenty-four hours, to erase the tension between us. I felt so guilty that Raleigh didn't seem as important anymore. All the way home I had debated telling Buddy what I had done and finally decided against it; the only purpose it would serve would be to hurt him. Maybe I was adopting what Buddy said about Raleigh for myself: it was history.

Buddy sat with me while I picked at my plate. I told him about the ride with Ralph and some of the storm stories I heard in the lounge. I knew I was talking nervously and too much, but I couldn't stop. Buddy sat back in his chair listening, his eyes slightly narrowed as they are when he concentrates on the movement of a ball. He said nothing. Finally, I asked him if anything had happened while I was gone. "The battery in my car died yesterday. I didn't get home until after seven. The yo-yo who put in the new battery dislodged the air filter hose. I discovered it today when I checked the oil."

Although I honestly didn't care, I asked him where he bought the battery simply to engage him.

"Sears," he said.

He didn't say more until I started upstairs with a bag from the outlet mall. "What did you buy?"

I showed him the robe and the nightgown. "I had to get toiletries, too," I said. "Avery paid for it all."

Then Buddy's eyes met mine. The hurt in them was so bare I had to blink and look away. "You slept with him, didn't you?"

I started to cry. "I'm sorry... I'm so sorry... It should never have happened... When I talked to you last night you were so cold... You sounded as if you didn't care if I ever came home... I was devastated."

"That's neat," Buddy said caustically. "Blame me! And he was there to comfort you."

"It wasn't like that... He'd been waiting for me... The toilet in my bathroom wasn't working... I was supposed to use his bathroom but I called you first..."

"I don't want to hear any more!" Buddy shouted.

Then he left. I heard the door slam and the garage door open and close while I sat on the stairs, weeping.

He was gone for over three hours. When I stopped crying, I washed my face and put on a nightgown and an old bathrobe. Then I went into the living room, where I sat in the semi-darkness waiting for him.

I don't know where he went. When he came back I could tell by the sag of his shoulders that he was exhausted. He looked dreadful; his skin was gray. "I can't handle it," he said. "It's the one thing I just can't handle. I've had a lot of opportunities—dozens over the years—and I never cheated on you. I never betrayed you, not once."

"Except for this one time, I never did, either. You know that. I wish it had never happened. I wish I could make it up to you."

"It's too late."

"What do you mean?"

"One of us has to leave, at least for a while."

"No, Buddy!" I cried.

That night he slept in Steve's room. I tried to talk to him in the morning. "Please, Buddy," I begged, "listen to me."

"Right now I can't stand seeing you or hearing you."

The expression on his face made me catch my breath: I had seen it once before, the day he told his father he would never have anything to do with him again.

And he never did.

I was crying so hard I didn't know or care what I

was putting into my suitcase. I just threw things in and left the house with no idea of where I was going.

Without thinking I drove in the direction of the cottage. By the time I realized where I was it was snowing hard. If I'd been thinking clearly, I would have turned back. The electricity to the cottage had been shut off, the water pipes drained; there was no food and no central heat. And if that weren't sufficient reason to turn around, I had a ferocious headache and my throat hurt.

None of it mattered. I kept going.

Buddy

I never expected to see Hoot or any of the guys I played with after I left baseball, so when the telephone rang one night after the holidays and I heard a man say, "Hey, Buddy, you wanna talk some ball?" I was astonished. Those are the most common words in baseball, but only one man could spin them together in quite that way. Hearing Hoot's voice after so many years was like suddenly having a door opened that I thought was permanently closed. Memories came rushing back, a whirlwind of memories that made my head spin. When Hoot told me he had lung cancer, the sadness I felt was as sharp as my happiness moments earlier at hearing his voice. For me it was the emotional roller coaster ride of baseball all over again.

After so many years nothing changed for Ginger, either. When I told her that I invited Hoot for dinner she got a tight look on her face, little lines of irritation hugging the corners of her eyes and mouth, the same lines she had in Raleigh except these were deeper because she's older. "Can't we take him out to dinner?" she said, sighing as though she were exhausted.

For the second time that night I was astounded. I had told her Hoot was alone in town and he was dying, and she wanted to take him to a restaurant like an unwelcome guest. Even if she was tired—Ginger always goes overboard for the holidays, pushing herself to do more than is necessary or expected—she would have cooked for the two of us anyway. She had no trouble preparing a meal for Avery Laird at the last minute at the end of a long work day, so I didn't think asking her to add an extra plate to the table and a little more food to the pot for Hoot was expecting too much.

Ginger spent about a half hour with Hoot before I got home. It didn't occur to me to ask what they talked about. Ginger disappeared into the kitchen as soon as I had my coat off, and except for eating with us, she left us alone for the rest of the evening so we could "Talk some ball."

And did we talk! Time slipped away faster than a missed line drive through an outfielder's hands. Hoot told me what happened to some of the fellows I played with, which guys were tapped for the majors and which ones hung around the minors until they got the message that they weren't going anywhere. Getting tapped for the majors had nothing to do with being a smart player. We talked about the time an outfielder named Eddie, who hit a triple in the ninth inning, left the baseline and went to the dugout thinking his hit had won the game. He was waiting to be congratulated when he was tagged out; his triple had only tied the game. We called him Early Eddie until he escaped the Raleigh Caps for an AA team. Then there was the rookie pitcher who was asked one night by a reporter if he thought he'd have trouble pitching because of the drizzle and heavy mist. "Naw," said the pitcher, whose name was Bobby, "we can lose in any weather." Bobby flew up to the majors after one season with the Caps, but he didn't last. And we shook our heads over Sal Capizzi, a smart guy and a solid player who should have made it to the majors and didn't. Sometimes there is no explanation. As baseball players say, "I'd rather be lucky than talented."

There were some things we didn't say, at least I didn't say. I remembered Hoot's generous friendship, how he visited me every day in the hospital after I had surgery on my knee, how he commiserated with me when I was in a slump. I remembered how intense my time was on the Raleigh Caps–trying to play my best, striving to perform, perform, perform—and how Hoot's sense of humor, his wacky way of looking at things, made the intensity bearable. Hoot made me laugh and it was the laughter that got me through it.

Talking took its toll on Hoot. He struggled with a persistent cough and his color was chalky, but when I expressed my concern, he held up his hands— catcher's hands with enlarged knuckles from old breaks and a couple of twisted fingers—to stop my worry, and he kept on talking and coughing. I think we both knew that the report he would get from the doctors the next day would be negative and we wouldn't see each other again. It was a hard thing to know. Hoot's such a decent guy, and he was a damned good ballplayer, every bit as good as some who made it. To see him dying in what should have been the middle of his life after he had first achieved success was almost more than I could take. After I dropped him off at his hotel, I drove home wiping tears off my face.

At school the next morning I left word that I wanted to be paged if a Mr. Hooter called. I was in the middle of a geometry class when his call came. He told me that the verdict was indeed bad, that he had no more than three or four months at the most to live. I swallowed hard and told him that I was sorry. "Me, too," said Hoot. "But it sure was good to see y'all."

"It sure was," I said.

Getting through the remainder of the day was tough. I couldn't stop thinking about Hoot, and I suppose it was only natural that I was feeling my own mortality as well. It was one of those times when the world just doesn't make sense. At dinner that night I went on and on about Hoot, so consumed by my grief I didn't notice that Ginger hadn't touched anything on her plate. Ginger has a healthy appetite, which is probably what prodded her into becoming a great cook, so when she doesn't eat I know something is wrong. I asked and she let me have it.

While she and Hoot visited before I came home, Hoot told her that I quit baseball because I didn't want to get old on the bench. Apparently Hoot told her a story about a guy called Methuselah, who had been around forever. Ginger repeated what Hoot said, demanding to know why I had never told her about Methuselah and growing old on the bench. She wanted to know why I let her believe that I quit because of her.

I thought she was making a big deal out of nothing. I didn't even remember Methuselah, so I tried to brush the whole business off, which made her more upset. She sat at the kitchen table shaking with anger, demanding that I tell her the truth, a truth which consisted of her having no involvement in my decision to quit.

I couldn't tell her what she wanted to hear. Like it or not, I believed she was a factor, and when I said so, she became angrier. At that point I became angry, too. I told her to drop it, but she wouldn't; she took her position and she stayed there, not budging, even though we had once agreed that we would never talk about my quitting baseball again.

Over the years we'd had our share of disagreements, though none were really major. We usually had great reconciliations after big fights, sweet sexy rewards more than worth the price of battle, but this time there was no reconciliation. Ginger carried it on for days, taking it so far that she didn't even bother to tell me when the article she had written had been published, which hurt; we had always shared our successes. It also made me angry. Not telling me about the article set me up for embarrassment when our friends called to congratulate her. When I asked her why she didn't tell me, she dragged up baseball again, the one subject she knows is painful for me, and she wouldn't let go. Couples who have been married a long time can hit each other's vulnerable spots with deadly accuracy. Ginger was throwing darts, and I was the target. Now she was going too far, and I was getting tired of ducking.

I've always had good instincts. They're a gift, like good eyesight, nothing I can take credit for. When Ginger told me that she was going to Niagara Falls with Avery Laird, I had a feeling in my gut it would be disastrous, but I couldn't say anything because it would have only made her angrier. From the beginning I sensed that Laird's interest in her went way beyond real estate. The job he offered her—sixty thousand dollars a year with flexible hours so she could pursue her interest in writing—was the creation of a man who had more on his mind than buying and selling property, particularly a man with a reputation as tough as Laird's for demanding and getting his money's worth. But she resented it every time I questioned his motives, so after a while I kept my doubts to myself. Then he had dinner at our house. I thought it was the perfect time to ask him what his intentions were; doing the unexpected often elicits the most honest responses.

"My intentions?" he said with an odd smile, as though he weren't sure he'd heard me correctly.

"Yes," I said, "your intentions."

He didn't hesitate. "I intend to marry your wife."

Ginger thought he was joking and laughed. I laughed, too, but I watched him. I saw how he gazed at her from across the dining room table, listening intently to every word she uttered, his eyes the bright, eager green of street lights, and I knew that he meant it. So Ginger went to Niagara Falls with him and there was a snow storm and she wasn't in her room when I called her. And then she came home and talked fast like she always does when she's nervous or when something is really wrong. I sat at the kitchen table so heartsick I had trouble hearing what she was saying. I saw her mouth move and her hands gesture, but what I really saw was Ginger in bed with Avery Laird. I couldn't stand it, I just couldn't stand it. My throat constricted and my temples started to throb.

I drove to the high school and ran around the gym for hours, thoughts circling and circling in my head as my feet circled the shiny gym floor, nothing making sense. I thought of all the women I could have had over the years, ripening high school girls thrusting their new breasts at me, pretty young fans trailing after the team when I played baseball, women I met at parties who wanted to make it with a jock, teachers I worked with who were lonely and frustrated. And I didn't touch one of them, not once. It isn't that they weren't interesting or appealing or downright sexy. They were all those things and more, but I loved Ginger and I knew that if I started to play I might not be able to stop. Ginger and I had been sweethearts since she was sixteen, and with the exception of a brief period before we were married, I never strayed. Even that wasn't straying, not really. Ginger was hundreds of miles away, I was lonely, and I met Flashlight Annie, who was as spicy and delectable as good Carolina barbecue.

I met Annie the first year I played for the Raleigh Caps. Everything was new and strange and not what I expected. After playing four years of college ball, I thought I could step right into the minors, show my stuff for a while, and then get tapped. But after I was up to bat a few times, I knew it wasn't going to happen that way. Although they didn't use radar guns to clock the speed of pitches then like they do now, the guy who pitched to me the first time I was up to bat had a fastball that must have been going over ninety miles an hour. He also had a wicked slider. I was out before I knew what happened. College ball wasn't like this, and the reason didn't take long to dawn on me: the guys in the minors were all hand-picked for their potential. Like me, they were strong players who wanted to get to the majors, except I was no longer so sure I would get there. Instead of putting me on third base, which I had always played, the manager decided to place me in the outfield. I saw my college batting average of .349 start to slide, I was playing in an unfamiliar position, and I was getting daily letters from Ginger saying how proud she was of me and telling me how sure she was that I was doing well. It wasn't an easy time.

I hit my first homer in the minors the night I met Annie. It was a home game, and she was with a group of girls that always seemed to be waiting outside the clubhouse after games. "Hey, that was some homer you hit," she said. "I hope you heard me cheering."

"Was that you?" I said, bending to get a better look at her. She was a tiny-boned Southern girl who had large dark eyes set in a pixy face. "It's hard to see who's cheering."

"Maybe next time I'll bring a flashlight so you know who it is."

"Then I certainly won't miss you," I said. "But that means I have to hit another homer."

"You will," she said with a smile that was full of mischief.

She told me that her name was Annie. "I'll look for you, Annie," I said.

At the next home game I hit another homer, and as I was trotting around the bases, relishing each step, I happened to glance up at the stands and saw a circling flashlight. Annie, I thought. I smiled and waved. The flashlight waved back. From that night on all the guys on the team called her Flashlight Annie.

Annie was waiting for me after the game, a big grin on her face. "You saw me!" she said.

"I couldn't miss you."

She held up a big chrome flashlight. "It's my daddy's," she said. "Ain't it something?"

"It sure is," I said.

Some of the fellows were taking girls out for beers, and on an impulse I invited Annie. At the time I believed she brought me luck, and I didn't think taking her would do any harm. But I was young and so was Annie, and when she gazed up at me with those huge dark eyes, I told myself that Ginger was hundreds of miles away and wouldn't know the difference. And she never did.

The house where I was rooming, an old Southern Victorian monster, had a set of back stairs. Hoot, who also roomed there, would check to see that the coast was clear and I'd sneak Annie up. She was only eighteen, but she had great instincts and no inhibitions. Annie used the flashlight in ways the manufacturer never dreamed of.

Oh, she was something, Flashlight Annie!

Mid-season, I tore the ligaments in my knee. It happened in a freak accident on a night the grass was slick after a rain. I went after a fly ball. The third baseman went after it, too. When I leaped for it, he tried to stop and instead skidded into me, twisting my leg as I was coming down. The pain in my knee was unbelievable. It was the end of the season for me and Flashlight Annie.

She was there the following year, waiting for me after the first game, her smile so sweet and happy that it broke my heart to see the hurt in those huge dark eyes when I told her I was married. "I'll flash for you anyway," she offered.

"Thanks, but maybe it would be better if you didn't," I said.

After that whenever I got a hit I tried not to look up at the stands. Annie's flashlight had helped light my way through that rough first season; I didn't realize how much I'd miss it until it was gone.

Having Ginger in the stands was different. Though she cheered for me as hard as Annie did, she was also anxious, especially when there were scouts present. Some nights her anxiety drifted down on me like a rain shower. Then if I played well—hit a triple or a homer or made a difficult catch—some of the tension would leave my body. But I was always conscious of Ginger being there, of her watching the play as if it were a poker game and my performance our ante.

If I'd had any sense, I wouldn't have had Ginger come to Raleigh, but I was young and in love and newly-married. Annie was a toy, cute and fun to play with, but Ginger was my life. I'd been on my own since I was eighteen, when my mother died and I moved out of my father's house. Ginger was my only family even before we were married; she and baseball were all that mattered to me. Her parents gave us a big wedding before I left for my second season, and Ginger joined me after she finished her exams for her last semester in college. I knew it wasn't going to be easy from the expression on Ginger's face when I brought her to Mrs. Moneypenny's boarding house, where I'd rented a room for us, but I had no idea it would be as difficult as it turned out to be.

I don't think Ginger blinked for at least five minutes after we arrived at Mrs. Moneypenny's. She just looked and looked and looked, as though by looking really hard she might see something else. She didn't say a word; those unblinking eyes said it all. I kind of knew how she felt. Some of the facilities the team had to use for out-of-town games made me stare in surprise when I saw them—dirty, foul-smelling places that had primitive showers and one or two toilets in stalls without doors. Mrs. Moneypenny's was no palace, but it was clean.

Ginger's reaction to the Southern summer wasn't much different from her reaction to Mrs. Moneypenny's. Again, she didn't complain. Instead, with each day's heat and humidity Ginger seemed to wilt a little more. After less than a month in Raleigh, my bride lost her sparkle.

Sparkle is the word that best describes Ginger, and her sparkle is what originally attracted me. There is a brightness in her eyes and an effervescence in her smile that I've never seen in another woman. When Ginger is happy her face is full of warmth and light, a radiance that is dazzling. Ginger sparkles in her baby pictures, in our wedding photographs, in snapshots of us with the boys as they were growing up. But in Raleigh that luminous face was gone; it was as if the girl I'd married had vanished.

She tried not to show how miserable she was, which made it impossible for me to suggest that she go back to Clinton Falls for the remainder of the season without hurting her. As I circled the gym remembering those days, I saw how out of place she was in Raleigh. Compared with the other wives and girl friends, Ginger was a thoroughbred among farm horses, so bright and sleek it was as if she were from a different species. Maybe it was my fault. Maybe I should have looked carefully at the situation before I put her in it, but as I said, I was young and in love, a condition that pretty much precludes thinking.

An athlete's psyche is as fragile as the thinnest glass. I've seen guys who wouldn't step onto a ball field unless their socks were put on inside out or their pockets were loaded with lucky charms arranged in a certain order. My first year in the minors I was at a card game in which a beefy guy named Willie accused a fellow called Token of cheating. Token, who had a sharp nose and a fast tongue, denied he'd cheated and started to joke about Willie being a sore loser, which got Willie really hot. "You ain't gonna get a hit your next twenty times at bat," Willie said, "and that'll prove you're a cheat!" Token's eyes bugged and everyone got very quiet. Someone suggested that Token return Willie's money and let bygones be bygones, but both men refused. What was said couldn't be taken back. The next day Token looked spooked when he went up to bat, and we all watched him blow some easy balls and strike out. And Willie sat on the bench nodding to himself at how he'd fixed Token good. Any fool knew Token would be hitless his next nineteen times up at bat, and since we were all fools, we were careful around Willie for the rest of the season; a ballplayer who would curse a teammate was capable of anything.

As the season progressed, Raleigh became an endurance contest for Ginger and she started to worry in earnest. She worried about how I was playing and about our future. The more she worried, the harder she tried to hide it because she worried most about how she was affecting me. But I knew Ginger almost as well as I knew myself. I knew when her smile was real and when it was brave. I knew what she was thinking and I caught her worry like it was a cold and I went into a slump.

There isn't a ballplayer who hasn't been in a slump at one time or another. Some guys believe slumps last for two weeks, but I've seen them go shorter and go longer. No matter how long they last, they're hell living through. My slump lasted less than two weeks, but during that time I was as uptight as Ginger gets a week before her period. I did all the usual things—went to a lighter bat, then to a heavier bat, then moved the bat up on my shoulder, then moved it down—but nothing helped. I went to batting practice every day and couldn't hit worth a damn. Things got so tense between Ginger and me that we started picking at each other; she was as uptight about the slump as I was, and that made me even more uptight.

Sal Capizzi got me out of it. He happened to notice that I was standing in the middle of the batter's box, which made me lunge at the ball off-balance. I moved up in the box and the slump was over.

Besides Hoot, the fellow I was friendliest with on the team was Sal. He played right field, and he had one of the top home run records in the minors. A good fielder, a strong hitter and a team player, Sal had all the talent for the big leagues, but he never made it. When I met him he had bounced from team to team for nine or ten years. No one could figure it out; there was absolutely no explanation. He was a perfect example of why ballplayers say, "I'd rather be lucky than talented."

Sal was transferred to the Raleigh Caps the year I started as a rookie. Our friendship developed quickly, probably because we were both new to the team; at times he was like a mentor, helping me find my way. As I got to know him better and saw how well he played, his presence on the Caps began to puzzle me: Sal had his pride, too much pride to be playing on a Class B team after so many years in baseball. I wondered about it until I hurt my knee and landed in the hospital. Sal came to visit on a Saturday night, which was a surprise; he was a big, handsome guy who could have had a harem of Southern women if he'd wanted one. "There must be a lot of disappointed ladies in Raleigh tonight," I said.

Sal laughed. "I was busy after the game this afternoon. This is just a breather. Someone's waiting for me now. I told her I'd be late."

"At this pace you won't last the season," I kidded.

He shrugged. "A fellow has to take his pleasure when he can."

He told me that his marriage was unhappy. "I put a ring on her finger and she turned from an angel into a shrew. It was like something out of a nightmare. I don't know how I'll escape her when I can't play ball anymore. Some nights I dream I can't play and I wake up in a cold sweat. Can you imagine: a cold sweat in this heat? Only my wife can inspire that."

I asked him why he didn't divorce her. "We both come from old-fashioned Catholic families," he said. "Our people don't divorce. They suffer."

After so many years I could still see the pain that shot across his face when he said *suffer,* pain so deep I had to look away.

But then Sal disappeared and I saw Ginger with Laird, and I sank to the gym floor, my own pain pulling me apart. Never, not even when my mother died, had I felt such hurt, such incredible agony. There was no one I trusted more than Ginger, no one I loved more. I couldn't handle it.

And that is what I told her after I showered and dressed and went back home. I said I couldn't handle it, that one of us would have to leave. She cried, as I knew she would, but it didn't upset me the way her crying usually does. I couldn't let her touch me—not her pleas, not her tears—or I would fall apart.

I was up most of the night tossing in Steve's room. Nothing changed in the morning. I still couldn't bear to look at her, to hear her voice, and when I told her, she saw that it was true and she went to the basement to get a suitcase.

During the winter I play tennis in an indoor center on Saturday mornings. My game was scheduled for nine thirty, but I didn't want to be home when Ginger left so I threw my tennis clothes and sneakers into a gym bag and pulled out of the driveway at about eight fifteen. It was miserably cold and the sky was a flat milky gray. I drove to a coffee shop for breakfast, which was a mistake. Although I took an end booth and sat with my back to the door, people recognized me anyway and came to my table to say hello. The pancakes I ordered got cold on my plate—the one mouthful I took tasted like sand—so I drank my coffee and left. Trying to play tennis was an even bigger mistake, really unfair to the guys and hell for me. It was impossible to concentrate. I played so badly I couldn't wait to get out of there.

It was snowing hard as I drove home so I had to pay attention to the roads, which were becoming treacherous, but when I pulled into the garage and saw Ginger's empty space next to mine, a lump rose in my throat. I turned off the ignition, put my head against the steering wheel, and wept.

When I finally went inside, I saw the light on the answering machine, which is at the end of a long counter in the kitchen, blinking hysterically. Blink. Blink. Blink. Blink. Blink. I pressed the message button and listened:

Hi Ginger,
It's Sue. Do we still have a date for tonight? Art gave up on his diet, so he doesn't care where we eat as long as they serve big portions! Give me a ring when you get a chance so we can make reservations.

Ginger,
I haven't spoken with you since Wednesday night. I hope you returned safely from Niagara Falls and that everything is fine. Please call before twelve thirty if you can. I'll be at Fay Wyman's house this afternoon for lunch and bridge if the weather holds.
(Thelma, Ginger's mother)

Hi Ginger,

It's nine forty-five. The weathermen are predicting a disaster, but I don't want to believe them. Are we still on for lunch? How do you feel about trying the new Chinese restaurant on Westfield? I bumped into Fran Archer yesterday and she raved about it. Damn, I just looked out the window and saw snowflakes. I hope whatever is coming will hold off for a while. I'm going to run out to do some errands, maybe hit a supermarket just in case. I should be back before eleven thirty.

(Jane Thacker)

Hi Mom,

I hear you're in for a storm that's supposed to be a bruiser. If you aren't out getting groceries now, make a run for it! I'm going to leave soon to study at the library, so don't call me back. I'll try to get in touch with you later.

Zack's remark about making a run for it forced a smile. When the boys were young, Ginger didn't believe a storm prediction and decided not to bother going to the store. We were socked-in for four days and were out of milk for three of them. From that time on she hurried to the supermarket whenever there were storm warnings; her speedy (and what sometimes turned out to be unnecessary) response got to be a family joke, as did our cupboards stocked with food. Zack used to say we could survive a winter in Alaska with what was in Ginger's cupboards.

The smile vanished when I noticed that Ginger had left her cell phone charger, which was plugged into the socket below the one used by the answering machine. She was upset when she left; there were probably other things she needed that she'd forgotten as well. All I could do was hope she was in a safe, warm place and that she would get in touch with us so we would know she was all right.

I decided to check the refrigerator, not that it would make any difference because I had no intention of going out again. Ginger usually goes grocery shopping at the end of the week, so there wasn't much to look at—a few eggs, less than a half quart of milk, a nearly empty bottle of white wine, a couple of cans of beer, some apples and oranges and lettuce and celery in the crispers; there was also cheese, as well as butter, salad dressings, several kinds of mustard, etc. With what was in the cupboards and the freezer, I could last through a blizzard with no problem.

My immediate dilemma was how to handle the telephone calls. Since the storm was raging now, a full show with howling winds and white-outs, I figured that I could ignore all of the messages except for Ginger's mother, who was probably sitting at home worrying. I knew the kind and decent thing to do would be to call her, but I couldn't think of anything to say that would be comforting, or even reassuring. I wasn't about to tell Thelma what had happened and I didn't know where Ginger was, so there really wasn't much I could do except put the answering machine on again and hope that Ginger would call Thelma later. I turned up the volume on the machine so I could hear callers as they were leaving their messages, but after Thelma called again, shaky-voiced with worry, I turned the volume down. Jane called several more times, also concerned, as was Zack when he called late in the day and got the machine. I returned his call Saturday night hoping he'd be out so I could leave a message. Zack is the most sensitive member of our family; sometimes I think he has a special radar because he sees what we miss, and he always seems to know and do what is needed. If he were in, he'd want to talk to Ginger and that would be a problem. I'd never lied to Zack and didn't want to start. Fortunately, he was out. I left a message wishing him luck on his exams.

The storm was over Saturday night, and by Sunday night I was bouncing off the walls. The telephone rang all day Sunday, Jane again (and again) and other friends. Thelma didn't call, so I figured that Ginger must have gotten in touch with her. Listening to the messages helped keep me sane. All day I walked from room to room, unable to find a place for myself, unable to concentrate on anything, even the play-offs. I didn't give a damn who won. Besides the telephone messages, the only thing that held my interest was listening to radio and television reports on road conditions. If I'd been allowed and knew how to operate a snow plow, I would have cleared every street in town to ensure that the schools would be open on Monday. I didn't know what I'd do if I had to stay home another day. Ginger was everywhere in the house—around every corner, in every room—and each time I saw her she was with Avery Laird. Although I tried not to, I couldn't stop wondering if she actually was with Laird. I didn't want to believe that she'd go to him, but it was a possibility: the storm started soon after she left, and I knew she wasn't with Jane or her mother. For the first time in twenty-seven years I didn't know where Ginger was, and although I couldn't admit it to myself, I was the one who felt lost.

Clinton Falls probably has the best street crews in the country because they get so much practice. We get dumped on all the time, one lake-effect snowstorm after another, and the crews fan out after each storm like a highly-specialized Army troop dedicated to their mission of reclaiming the streets. Eighteen inches of snow fell on Saturday, and on Monday the town was open and ready for business again, the streets plowed, salt spread to melt the ice and rust the cars. Glad to escape, I left the house looking forward to a day of teaching classes in which there were kids who weren't interested in learning, kids who were troubled, kids who were on drugs, kids who were raised on television whose eyes glazed as they sat back in their seats waiting for me to be as entertaining as MTV.

Maybe I made it sound worse than it is, though everything I said is true, and I'm one of the lucky ones because I have some classes in which I teach geometry and eleventh year math to college-bound students. English and history teachers who have a general mix of kids in their classes have it much harder than I do; they have to contend with kids barely able to read who have passed through the system year after year, kids who don't want to be in school, kids whose kicks come from disrupting classes and making teachers miserable. Although they won't admit it, some of the teachers are afraid of the kids, especially female teachers I've seen spending hours over-preparing for classes to make sure they'll be able to keep the kids occupied every minute.

Still, I like teaching, not as much as coaching, but I do like it. There is the challenge of getting kids interested in a subject they are taking only because it is required for college admission. There is the satisfaction of seeing a student who has floundered for weeks, possibly months, finally begin to understand the concepts of geometry. There is the pleasure of being with bright young people, of seeing them grow before your eyes, both mentally and physically, and knowing that you are a part of it. And finally, there is the pleasure of the subject itself, the clean logic of math. A guy named Bill Veeck once said, "Baseball is almost the only orderly thing in a very unorderly world." The same could be said for the step-by-step proof of a theorem.

I got into teaching because of baseball. I needed to support myself off-season, and since I didn't want to sell insurance with Ginger's father or work in a store or an office, I tried substitute teaching and liked it right away. I was a math major in college so I had a subject that was in demand, and my years playing sports opened the door to coaching. For me, the real pleasure is in coaching, though it gets harder and more frustrating every year. The Beaver Cleaver America is long gone. Today kids come from homes where both parents work; almost half the kids come from broken homes. The community has changed, too. When I was growing up there was community involvement, community pride; people in Clinton Falls would turn out on Friday nights to see a game, and if a kid took a wrong turn, someone would let you know. Today people are self-focused, busy concentrating on their careers, on their life styles, on whatever happens to interest them at the moment. And then there are the twin plagues of drugs and alcohol. Booze has always been a problem, and drugs become more of a menace every day. Coke, crack, speed–there's a long list of them, and although they differ in chemical composition, they all accomplish the same thing: they pull good kids off the track, sometimes permanently. This year I battled hard to save the best inside linebacker I'd ever coached. Greg Shanley, a freckled kid who has a cowlick on top of his head like Dennis the Menace's, had so much going for him–sports, a solid academic record–he could have had his ticket to college paid in full and possibly a professional career in football as well. I knew he was in trouble and I tried my damndest, but I just couldn't reach him; neither could his teachers. We all saw him sliding and we couldn't catch him, we couldn't pull him back.

It's a terrible thing to see any kid go under, but to see it happen to a kid with Greg Shanley's abilities, it's devastating. I kept thinking that I could have tried something else, that I could have done something differently. Rationally, I know it wasn't my failure: Shanley comes from a broken family and was on his own most of the time. But I was his coach, and the business of a coach is to help kids be the best they can be, to help them realize their potential.

I lost Shanley. The team lost Shanley, too. He was a field leader, and without him the defense fell apart. At the time Ginger thought I was upset because the team started losing. I don't like to lose, no one does, but it wasn't simply a matter of a final score. The kids on the defense believed that Shanley was the necessary part that made their engine work. I had to prove to them that they could be winners without him. It was a struggle, but we made it. I couldn't handle it any other way. When I was in high school, I had letters in three sports: football, basketball, and baseball. My father never attended a game I played in, not one, or any assembly in which I was given an award. He had no time for me, so my high school coaches gave me the attention and encouragement he didn't give. It probably sounds corny, but each time I help a kid I'm paying those coaches back.

I get more than I give. It's a pleasure to watch the improvement in kids through a season, to see them develop self-discipline, sportsmanship, and pride in full effort. There are few things more gratifying than witnessing positive growth and knowing that you are a part of it. After over twenty-five years in this business, I see fellows I've coached all over Clinton Falls, men who greet me with smiles and outstretched hands. It's great to be greeted like that, it really is.

No one at school greeted me with a smile on the Monday after the snowstorm. The kids were disappointed that the schools were open, as were most of the teachers, so the building was filled with grumpy people resenting where they were. Mid-winter is always tough; cabin fever starts to set in and everyone's touchy, their edges a bit frayed. But being at school was a damn sight better than being at home, sulking kids and gloomy colleagues included. Even the smell of the place, the over-ripe odor of brown-bag lunches stuck in lockers and the stale scent of dusty chalk trays, was welcome.

Jane surprised me with a visit late in the

afternoon. Somehow she managed to get up the front steps, which I made a mental note to take care of and promptly forgot. She stayed on the hall rug, either because she didn't want to take her boots off or because I made no gesture inviting her to step further. She was wearing a long dark fur coat that looked expensive. "I called here all weekend and left messages on the machine, and I called Laird Enterprises this morning," she said, her brown eyes locking squarely with mine. "Where's Ginger?"

Jane isn't commanding, but she is direct, so straightforward that it's nearly impossible to look away if she's got you in her sights. "I don't know," I said.

Shocked by my answer, she shifted her gaze to the snow melting off her leather boots. "I came here worried and now I don't know what to say."

I didn't know what to say either, so we stood there in an awkward silence until she asked me how long Ginger had been gone. "Since Saturday," I said. "I'd appreciate it if you didn't mention this to anyone. Ginger would, too."

"Does her mother know?"

"I'm not sure, and I wouldn't want to upset her by asking."

She nodded her agreement. "What about the boys?"

I shook my head.

Jane sighed, a compassionate sigh that made me realize I must have looked as sad as I felt. She reached for my hand and squeezed it. "I'm sure things will work themselves out," she said. "If you talk to Ginger or see her, please give her my love. I'm supposed to leave for Florida on Wednesday, but I'll cancel my plans if she needs me."

After Jane left, I thought about friendship. I wondered if any of the guys I'd played sports with for years would cancel a trip for me. I remembered how Jane had come running to Ginger for comfort and support when Cal wanted a divorce. I had occasionally felt that Jane had taken advantage of Ginger's generous nature, and I didn't want her to get involved. Now I saw it differently. I recalled times I'd overheard Ginger and her friends sharing confidences, intimate details of their lives that would make men squirm with embarrassment, and thought that this sharing must help them bond in a way that men don't. I have friends, good friends, but I don't have the relationship with any of them that Ginger has with Jane. My best friend is Ginger, and I stood in the hall for a long time after Jane left feeling more alone than I'd ever felt in my life.

Again on Tuesday afternoon I had a surprise visitor. At about four fifteen the doorbell rang. The bell reminded me that I hadn't taken care of the front steps, and as I went to the door I promised myself to clean them before someone broke a leg and sued. When I opened the door, however, my promise was forgotten.

I never thought I'd want to kill a man no matter what he did, but when I saw Avery Laird, I went berserk. My reaction was visceral—beyond thought, beyond reason, beyond sense and sanity. There he was on my doorstep, dapper in a gray wool coat and hat, the shark who seduced my wife, and I, who always prided myself in being rational, couldn't get to him fast enough. "You bastard!" I said, pushing open the storm door. My fist flew into his jaw.

He fell backward down the steps. No sooner had he landed than I was straddling him; there was a stab of pain in my knee when it met his ribs. "You fucking bastard!" I cried, pounding him until my knuckles were slippery with blood.

Somehow Laird managed to land a lucky punch. I heard the bone in my nose crack and felt an explosion of pain as I fell sideways. Laird struggled to his feet. "Where is Ginger?" he demanded, grabbing me by the hair. He yanked my head back. "Where is she?"

My head swirled. "I don't know."

Laird yanked my head back further, as though testing to see if I was telling the truth. Blood was dripping from gashes on his forehead, chin and cheek. Apparently satisfied, he let go of me and started walking toward his car, a black Mercedes parked in the driveway. Rage pushed me to my feet and I tackled him. Then it happened: something inside me snapped. My hands went to his throat, my thumbs to his windpipe. His face was turning color when a voice behind me said, "Hey, Mr. Middleton, are you going to kill him?"

It was the newsboy, watching with wide-eyed interest. I loosened my grip and reached for a paper.

Laird was gasping and coughing when I went into the house. My face, hands and clothes were bloody; my nose, which was throbbing wickedly, was still bleeding. I sat in the kitchen with an ice pack on my nose until the bleeding was down to a trickle, then called Pete Gilmore's office. It was almost five o'clock. A young-sounding receptionist answered. "Is

Dr. Gilmore in?" I said.

"He's with a patient," she said.

"This is Buddy Middleton. Please tell him I'm coming right over. I have a broken nose."

I hung up before she could reply, which was rude but necessary. I was sure that if Pete got the message he would see me so I wouldn't have to go to the emergency room at Sweet Memorial, where I would probably bump into at least one person I knew. Vernon Sweet Memorial is the community hospital that Clinton Falls natives use for minor injuries and illnesses and routine surgical procedures; only people from out of town, the indigent, and the seriously ill go to the university hospital. Eventually I'd have to explain my nose, but I wanted to put if off as long as possible.

Before I left I changed my clothes, and washed my face and hands. Still, I was a sight. Despite the ice pack, my nose was spreading like putty across my face, and two shiners were blooming around my eyes. As I drove to Pete Gilmore's office, I tried to figure out something I could tell him. Nothing inspiring came to mind, so I decided to say as little as possible, maybe allude to a gym accident and leave it at that. Pete wouldn't push if I let him know he shouldn't; ours wasn't a particularly close friendship, but it was a long-standing one.

Pete and I have known each other since we were in grammar school. He was a short, scrawny kid who loved sports but was terrible at them. In high school he decided that, since he couldn't play, he would like to manage a team. Pete might have been picked by his math and science teachers, but there was no way any of the coaches would choose him. One day he asked me if I would plead his case when he heard there was an opening. "I really want to be the manager of the baseball team," he said. "Please, Buddy, you're my only chance."

I looked at him doubtfully. "Tell the coach I'll be great for team morale," he said. "I'll keep them laughing."

It was something Pete could do: he was slow on the field, but he had a quick, zany sense of humor. I told that to the coach. I also told the coach how much Pete wanted to be the manager. "He'll be good because no one wants it more than he does."

The coach saw my point and Pete became the manager. And he was as good as he promised he'd be.

Over the years Pete filled out, lost most of his hair, and became the best and busiest plastic surgeon in Clinton Falls. He also seemed to lose most of his zaniness. Occasionally I wondered if, because of his success, he didn't feel the need to be funny anymore. But he was still a decent guy, and I had no doubt when I got off the elevator and opened the door to his suite of offices that he would be there waiting for me.

The receptionist didn't have to ask who I was. "Mr. Middleton," she said rising as I approached her desk. She was in her twenties, dark-haired and exceptionally pretty. I noticed that she was small, just about the right size for Pete, but before I had a chance to pursue that thought, she had efficiently passed me along to an X-ray technician, who took pictures of my nose and then led me to an examining room. Pete hurried in carrying the X-rays. "You're lucky," he said, extending his hand. "It's a clean break, should heal nicely. How did it happen?"

"I didn't duck fast enough," I said, smiling to make light of it. "Guess I'm getting old."

Fortunately, Pete didn't question me further. He's always been a gossip, and his news, which was the reason for his hurry, was far more interesting to him than my broken nose. "I hate to rush," he said, working on me while he talked, "but a VIP is waiting for me in the emergency room. According to my resident, one of Clinton Falls' most prominent citizens was badly beaten up–multiple lacerations, loose teeth, a couple of broken ribs."

While he was speaking I cupped my hands together, holding them palms up so he couldn't see my bruised knuckles. "I don't suppose you can tell me who it is?"

"Well," he said, "I really shouldn't, but... what the hell. I can trust you to keep it under your hat. It's the developer, Avery Laird. And it was no casual beating. There's evidence that whoever did it tried to choke him to death."

It was then that I felt the full impact of what I had done. "Has he said who it was?"

Pete shook his head. "Not a word. He's insisting upon absolute privacy; he said he'd sue the hospital if they notified the police or the media. Maybe I'll be able to get him to open up," he said, chuckling. "I heard a great joke at lunch today about a hooker and a hockey player that I can try on him."

He put his hand on my shoulder. "Sorry I have to rush off. Be sure you get an appointment before you leave. And give my best to Ginger."

"Thanks for seeing me."

"No problem," he said, hurrying out the door.

When I got into the car to go home, I started to shake. There was no doubt in my mind that if the newsboy hadn't come along, I would have killed Laird. No doubt whatsoever. I had been lucky, and the more I realized it the harder I shook. It was a while before I was steady again.

Driving home, I thought about what Pete had said about Laird not talking. I doubted that Pete's jokes would loosen Laird's tongue, not if he cared about Ginger as much as I believed he did. From what I could see Laird was dead serious about Ginger and would do nothing that would in any way affect her reputation, including report that he was nearly beaten to death by her husband. For one brief, irrational moment I wanted Laird to tell the police, proving me wrong. But I knew he wouldn't, and again the image of the two of them together that had haunted me for days came back, and I couldn't lose it.

Jane called soon after I got home. I still wasn't answering the phone, but I had the volume turned up on the answering machine and was monitoring all calls, hoping that one of them would be from Ginger. Jane's voice, cool and direct, came from the machine. "Buddy, this is Jane. I expect you to call me back."

I could have picked up the receiver, but then Jane would have known I was listening and I would have felt like an eavesdropper, so I waited about an hour before calling her back, glad she couldn't see the results of the fight: with a splint on my nose and two shiners, I looked like a mutant raccoon. Jane wanted to know if I'd heard from Ginger. When I told her that I hadn't, she said, "I'm really worried. This isn't like her."

"I'm sure she's fine," I said.

Actually, I wasn't sure that Ginger was fine, and I'd been alternately angry and worried since Monday night. It might seem ridiculous, but after twenty-seven years of marriage, I expected her to let me know where she was, even if I was the one who wanted the separation, and the fact that she hadn't let me know really had me pissed. At that point, as Laird had quickly discovered, my temper was ragged. I hadn't had a decent night's sleep since Friday and was beginning to feel hollow, more of a shell than a human being. After school I just wandered through the house until the next morning, sleeping intermittently wherever I happened to land. I stayed out of our bedroom as much as I could and didn't go near our bed, which Ginger had made before she left. I couldn't risk lifting off the bedspread, crawling under the covers, and placing my head on the pillow next to hers, where I might inhale the scent of her perfume.

Tuesday night was even worse than the previous nights. Between my throbbing nose, worrying about Ginger, and thinking about my fight with Laird, both what did happen and what might have happened, I was too busy to sleep. Finally, at six fifteen I called the principal and told him that I had an accident and wouldn't be coming in for the remainder of the week. I rarely take sick days, no more than one or two a year if any, so these weren't out of line.

I slept on and off for most of the day, and when Steve called Wednesday night, I was glad to talk to him. It was good to have some company. He asked for Ginger, and I told him she was out, which he accepted without further questions. We talked about his decision to accept an offer from a Boston law firm that had been courting him for a while. The Manhattan firm he'd worked for last summer offered him ninety-five thousand dollars, five thousand more than the Boston firm's offer, but he likes Boston better than New York. "It's a gut feeling, but I think I'll have a better opportunity in the Boston firm," he said.

"Then go for it," I said.

Later I thought about the salary he'd be earning, an obscene amount of money for a kid just out of school who knew practically nothing about practicing law. But then I thought of the money he would have been earning as a professional quarterback if the bones in his wrist hadn't been shattered, and the law firms' offers seemed paltry. It was quite a lesson in relativity. I'm not minimizing the ninety thousand dollars; it's more than I'll ever earn in a year. In the end, it isn't about money. It's about playing football, which Steve loved.

If Ginger had been home, she would have been thrilled with the law firms' offers and would have bubbled all night about the wonderful legal career Steve was embarking on. She didn't want him to play football and she never truly grasped how exceptional his talent was, a gift comparable to a great musician's or a fine artist's. Steve's gift wasn't just a combination of superior coordination and intelligence; what truly set him apart was his eyesight, the ability to see an entire playing field. It's difficult to explain other than to say he has a wider range of vision than the rest of us have, a kind of expanded peripheral vision. He was able to set up a play because he could see it all developing: when he threw to an empty spot, he knew it wouldn't be empty.

Steve was a toddler when I became aware of his extraordinary eyesight. Ginger and I had taken him to a park for a picnic; we were sitting on a blanket eating when suddenly he got up to go after a rabbit. He'd been sitting opposite me between Ginger's legs chewing on a piece of chicken, his hair gleaming white-blond in the sun, and I'd been talking to him. I knew I had his attention: his eyes were focused on me and mine were on him, but I didn't see that rabbit; neither did Ginger. It seemed impossible, so I tested him later while he was watching television. I rolled a ball at an angle that should have been out of his line of vision, and sure enough he went after the ball. I'll never forget it. He rolled the ball back to me while I stood there dumbfounded.

That night I told Ginger. "Remember how Steve went after the rabbit today? I tested him with a ball and he did it again!"

"Did what?"

'"He saw the ball and went after it!"

"That's normal."

"No," I said impatiently. "He shouldn't have been able to see the ball. He has exceptional vision!"

She had just begun to toilet train him, and before she put him to bed, he turned to look at me as I walked by the bathroom and squirted all over the place. "Then we'll have to make sure nothing distracts him so he pees straight into the toilet," she said.

Ginger always had a knack for putting things in their proper order.

Although she never said it, I know Ginger

thought I was living vicariously through Steve, that I encouraged him to play football because I thought he would have a good chance at a professional career. I admit I enjoyed talking to the college reps that came calling when he was in high school, and it certainly was a thrill to see him on national television quarterbacking for a Big Ten school, but most men would have felt the same pride and pleasure I did. What Ginger didn't understand, and what *I knew*, was what Steve was experiencing, the incredible high an athlete feels when his mind and body are perfectly focused, every cell working in absolute harmony. This ability to perform, this synchronization of mind and body and soul is what propels all athletes, and Steve's choice of football was as logical as the rungs in a ladder: it was the sport to which he instinctively went to best use his gifts. For him to play baseball, which Ginger would have preferred, would have been as big a waste as telling Michelangelo to pack his artist's brushes away and start painting plain ceilings with the flat wide brush of a house painter.

After Steve was injured and the doctors operated on him, I didn't have to look at Ginger's face to know that relief was written all over it when we were told he'd never play football again. My face must have looked as grim as death. I knew what playing meant to Steve. I knew how it felt to be close to a professional career, to the opportunity to play with the best of the best. Without question Steve would have made it: he had unlimited potential, the ability to develop into one of the greats. I walked out of the University of Michigan Hospital with a bitter taste in my mouth that comes back sometimes when I think of Steve and what he might have had, so I try not to think about it. There is no point in dwelling on what you can't change. But occasionally when I look at him, I wonder how he feels about what happened, and how he'll feel about it thirty years from now.

Zack surprised me by coming home late Thursday afternoon. I didn't expect him until the weekend and was dozing when I heard the door open. At first I thought it might be Ginger, but then he called, "Anyone home?" and I slumped back in my chair.

"In the family room," I said.

It's a straight trip from the front hall to the family room, and Zack, long and lanky, was looking down at me before I could blink twice. "Jesus, who hit you?" he said, dropping a bulging gray duffel bag on the rug.

"Avery Laird," I said, playing it straight. With Zack, there was no other way. "It was a lucky punch."

"Mom's boss?"

"Yup."

Zack looked at me again, a frown forming between his eyes, and then he glanced around the room and up at the kitchen, which overlooks the family room. There were newspapers and magazines on the floor where I had dropped them, and dirty dishes and glasses scattered on tables around the room; there was also quite a line-up of dirty dishes on the kitchen counters. "This place is a mess," Zack said. "Where's Mom?"

"I don't know."

"What do you mean *you don't know*?"

There was alarm in his voice and in his eyes, but if you didn't know him as well as I do, you couldn't hear or see it. Outwardly calm, he stood waiting for my reply. I felt terrible for him, and for me. "Honestly," I said, "I don't know where she is."

"How long has she been gone?"

"Since Saturday."

"What about Gram, does she know? Do I have to pull everything out of you piece-by-piece?"

He was agitated now, for which I couldn't blame him. "I haven't talked to Gram, but I have a feeling she might know because she hasn't called here since Saturday."

"Don't you want to know where Mom is? What's going on?"

"We've... kind of... separated for a while."

Zack waited for me to say more, but when he saw nothing was forthcoming, he picked up the duffel and went upstairs, stopping first to open the door to the garage where he saw Ginger's empty space. "I'm going to Gram's," he said when he came down. "I'll take care of the front steps before I leave."

He didn't come back until after nine. I knew how upset and worried he was, but I didn't expect him to be gone that long. As the hours passed I began to wonder if he was with Ginger. I wondered what she would tell him. Zack is an adult; he'd want the truth, but it wouldn't be easy. I figured that he'd eat with Thelma, so I had a peanut-butter-and-jelly sandwich, then picked up the newspapers and loaded the dishwasher. I was working on a second load of dishes when he came in. "Mom's at the cottage," he said, unzipping his jacket.

"How long has she been there?"

"Since the storm on Saturday," he said. He was looking at me carefully, studying me really, his face tight with concentration.

"There's no electricity, no water," I said, more to myself than to him. "Has Thelma talked to her?"

"No," he said. "Mr. Fowler called Gram."

Fowler is a handyman Ginger's parents have employed for years to take care of the cottage off-season. He's a busybody, so he's probably watching out for her, I thought. "I'm sure she's fine," I said.

"Well, I'm not," he said, "and neither is Gram, but she tried not to show how worried she is. I would have gone there tonight, but she made me promise that I'd wait until morning. She was afraid I might get stuck on the beach road."

"She's right," I said.

Zack, who isn't an early riser, was in the kitchen before seven, foraging for something to eat. He didn't have great choices. I had stopped at the supermarket after school on Monday, but most of that stuff was gone. He settled for a bowl of cornflakes. "Are you going to school today?" he said.

"No," I said, yawning. I'd spent a lousy night dozing in my chair in the family room. "I've taken the week off."

He poured what was left of the milk into his bowl. "Then you're coming with me to the cottage?"

"No."

I could see the disappointment in his eyes and wanted to tell him how sorry I was that he walked into this, but I couldn't say a word, so I sat with him, as inert as a potato, while he ate.

After he put his jacket on, he came back into the kitchen. I was still at the table. "I hope the reason you have for not coming with me is so good you'll be able to live with it."

His warning was almost an exact echo of mine to my father when I was younger than Zack. Suddenly caught in a flood of memories, I was only vaguely aware of him turning to leave and the door slamming behind him.

My mother died a few weeks before I graduated from high school. She had cancer, but I believe she really died of disappointment deeper than she could handle, and of the realization that the person who disappointed her—my father—was oblivious to what he'd done.

Her decline started after she had routine gall bladder surgery in September of my senior year. Gall bladder surgery wasn't as advanced then as it is today, with people coming and going from the hospital as if they're attending an afternoon matinee. Her surgery was at Sweet Memorial, and I visited her every day after football practice. On my third visit I noticed that her eyes were red and puffy, but when I asked her how she was feeling, she told me that she was fine. Despite her reassurance, she seemed so pale and sad that I intercepted the first nurse I saw when I left her room, a big comfortable-looking woman wearing a crisp uniform. I told her that I thought something might be wrong with my mother. "I think you should call the doctor," I said.

The nurse, who was nearly my height, put her hand on my shoulder and steered me down the hall away from my mother's room. "I shouldn't do this," she said. "I'm supposed to take care of the physical needs of patients, not interfere with their private lives, but I really feel for your mother, poor woman. I don't think her problem is medical."

That she would call my mother *poor woman* was not only alarming but a complete contradiction of the active, capable woman I knew. "What do you mean?"

"Your father has only visited your mother once since she's been here. Her eyes are always focused on the door, looking for him. This time, early evening, is the hardest because that's when the hospital starts filling up with visitors."

I can't recall if I thanked her. I remember feeling hot with shame and anger, and racing out of the hospital. I went straight home to wait for my father. I knew the wait would be a long one. He had just finished building what he was determined would be the best private laboratory in Central New York, and he had been consumed with getting everything set up to his satisfaction. My father wasn't a man who was easily satisfied. He was driven, a perfectionist who would work every hour in the twenty-four that make up a day to accomplish what he set out to do. His pharmacy, which dispensed only medication—no cosmetics or candy bars—had been written up in pharmacologic as well as popular magazines as a model, the finest of its kind. All my life I'd seen him forgo sleep, meals, relaxation, companionship—all the civilized, pleasurable aspects of being human— without noticing that he had missed anything. He belonged to a country club where he never played golf or tennis or sat by the pool; the membership was a convenience, a way of ensuring that he and my mother wouldn't have to wait for a table when they went out for dinner. He was more like a machine than a man, yet my mother loved him. She was so impressed with what he was accomplishing that she gratefully accepted the little time he gave her. I had practically no relationship with him at all; nor did my sister Ellen, who was five years older than me. His interest in us didn't seem to extend beyond our report cards; we were his offspring, and we were to do well. At the time of my mother's surgery he was particularly pleased with Ellen because she had just started her first year of medical school at Stanford. He had no interest whatsoever in sports and expected me to follow her example. Sitting alone in that big red brick house waiting for him, I wondered how anyone so different from me could be my father, but without question he was because I looked just like him.

He didn't come in until close to midnight. Hour after hour I waited, honing my anger, and he no sooner stepped inside than I speared him. "How many times have you visited Mom at the hospital?" I demanded.

"A couple," he said, his eyes flickering with annoyance.

"She's not doing well. Tonight she looked like she'd been crying."

"She knows how busy I've been. She understands."

"No," I said, my voice rising, "she watches the door all day, looking for you."

"Who told you that?"

"A nurse. I wanted her to call the doctor and she told me Mom's problem isn't medical. The problem is that her husband is too busy to visit her."

"Which damn nurse said that?" my father snapped, looking awake now.

"Why do you want to know? So you can have her fired for telling the truth?" I was shouting, angry and upset enough to do the unthinkable and take a poke at him.

"Go to bed," my father ordered.

His voice and expression were so cutting that I stepped back. "I hope you'll be able to live with what you're doing," I said before heading upstairs.

Nothing changed when my mother came home from the hospital: my father was still absorbed in the new laboratory, and my mother acted as though everything was fine. As the months passed, however, she didn't get completely well. She complained of vague abdominal pain, lost weight, and developed a chronic backache. Her doctor, who had been chosen by my father, attributed her complaints to a poor recovery from surgery. I wanted her to go to a different doctor, but she refused. "I've really tried to recover," she said, stung by the doctor's suggestion, with which my father concurred, that she was malingering. "I really have."

So in the shadows of two of the finest hospitals in the country my mother pretended that she was well while she was dying. Finally, in the spring, when the whites of her eyes turned yellow, my father saw that she was ill. She went to a new doctor and had surgery at the university hospital. The diagnosis was cancer of the pancreas. She was forty-six years old.

What I remember most about my last year in high school was watching my mother die and seeing my father do nothing about it until it was too late. The day after I graduated, I packed my things and moved into one of the dorms at the university. Clinton University took care of my room, board, and tuition for the next four years. All I had to do in return was play ball.

Ginger helped me move. My father came home as we were loading the last of my stuff into the car. When he asked me what was going on, I told him that I was leaving. "You won't miss me," I said. "You've always cared more about your business than your family anyway."

He squared his shoulders, gearing for a battle. "If your mother could see this, it would break her heart."

"That's impossible," I said. "You broke it long ago. Your neglect killed her and I'll never forgive you for it! I never want to see you again!"

Several years later he sold his business and moved to California to be near my sister. Ellen was more forgiving than I, more like my mother, I guess. In her last year in medical school she was killed in an automobile accident. My father sent me a letter by registered mail telling me that she had died and that he'd had her cremated. I held the letter in my hand for a long, long time, feeling the dryness of the paper, as dry as Ellen's ashes must have been. My sister and I weren't particularly close because of the difference in our ages, sex, and interests, but I loved her. She was all I had left of my family, of my mother. My eyes stinging, I crumpled the letter and burned it.

I hadn't thought about my father in years. Hearing my son warn me as I had once warned him was a shock, and the longer I waited for Zack to get in touch with me, the more agitated I became. I didn't intend to tell him the reason for my estrangement from Ginger, but I'd be damned before I'd let him think that I was in the wrong. *I had been wronged* and somehow he was going to know it.

Zack called at about eleven. "I'm at the university hospital," he said. "Mom's in intensive care. She has pneumonia."

I reacted to the university hospital like it was a red flag. "Why not Sweet Memorial? Whose decision was this?"

"Mine and Mr. Laird's. He got to the cottage right after I did. She's so sick we had to get her to a hospital fast, and the university hospital has a helicopter."

Laird. Now the field was full of red flags. "How did he know where she was?"

"He hired a detective to find her."

"Where is he now?"

"In one of the waiting rooms," Zack said. "He isn't allowed to see Mom. Only the immediate family can go in. She's in medical intensive care. It's on the third floor of the west wing. Can you call Gram?"

"I think you'd better call her."

"Should I tell her that you'll pick her up?"

"No." I didn't have the heart to tell him that I wasn't going to the hospital.

For the remainder of the day when I wasn't worrying about Ginger, I was stewing over Laird hiring a detective to find her, and then having the gall to sit in the hospital. Several times I put my jacket on to go see her, but I couldn't get past the door to the garage. By the time Zack got home shortly after ten, I was a banana. "How is she?" I said, pouncing on him.

"Not good." He looked beat; the muscles in his face were taut with worry. "She has pneumococcal pneumonia, and she's septic. She's on oxygen, and they're giving her IV antibiotics and fluids, as well as IV steroids to help her breathe better. One of her doctors put a needle through her chest wall to draw off fluid that was compressing her lung.

"I called Steve. The first flight he could get arrives early tomorrow morning. I'll pick him up at the airport and take him directly to the hospital."

I didn't doubt that Ginger was sick, but Zack seemed to be overreacting. "She'll be all right. She has a strong constitution."

"You don't understand how sick she is, do you?" he said, tears springing into his eyes. "She's septic. That means the infection has spread through her body. The doctors won't give her more than a fifty-fifty chance. *Mom could die.* I'd still be at the hospital if Gram weren't so exhausted. They said they'd call if there was any change in her condition."

Suddenly I had nothing to say. Zack, however, had plenty. "I don't know what happened here. I could guess, but it doesn't make any difference. The important thing is that you go to the hospital, that Mom sees you pulling for her."

"She'll have you and Steve and Gram."

"We're not enough. After Steve's wrist was smashed I did a lot of reading about rehabilitation, and about recovery in general. All the books I read seemed to say the same thing: desire is ninety-five percent of the battle. You're the most important person in Mom's life. You have to be there for her!"

I couldn't make any promises. "I'll think about it."

"YOU'LL THINK ABOUT IT!" Zack threw his hands into the air. "You don't have time to think about it! Do you remember when Jason Hamilton died? None of us saw it coming. We were just a group of kids going to a rock concert. We got to the concert early, but so did thousands of others; there was an ocean of kids waiting in that stifling August heat. When the gates finally opened, everyone surged forward in a human tidal wave. I felt crushed, I felt the air being pushed out of my lungs. Instinctively I knew I had to keep moving, I had to go with the force like it was a current, because if I hesitated, even for an instant, I'd be sucked under. Somehow I made it. We all did except for Jason.

"For a long time I thought about why Jason died. Why did it happen? Why? It was such a stupid, senseless waste! Jason was the quietest one in our group, the least likely to be in a fight because he believed that any problem could be reasoned out. But a tidal wave of kids at a rock concert isn't reasonable, and Jason, who always resisted force, was its victim. It was as if he were punished for being a good person, for being peaceful, for never having harmed anyone."

Zack took a deep breath, wiping tears off his face. Although I had tried to encourage him to talk about Jason when it happened, to open up instead of keeping the trauma locked inside him, he hadn't said a word until now. Over five years of silence. It was good for him to finally get it out, I thought. But he was far from finished.

"Jason's death still doesn't make sense and it never will, but I did learn something from it: his death showed me how chancy life is, how the world can change in the blink of an eye, and what's happened to Mom has proved it again. If I had stayed at school until the weekend as I had originally planned, or if Mr. Laird hadn't hired a detective, Mom might have died before we found her. I came home yesterday because a party scheduled for tonight was canceled. A party. *Mom could have died.*"

He looked hard at me. I thought of Laird at the hospital. "I don't know if I can do what you're asking."

Zack's face flushed with anger. "You're still making Mom come last, even if she might die! You're a real prize!"

I grabbed him by the shoulders. "What do you mean: *making Mom come last*?"

"You've always come first, and she's always stood around waiting for you. When you're done coaching and playing ball you give her your leftover time. And now you won't even give her that!"

"It isn't quite that simple," I replied, stung by what he said.

"Do you remember that Ernie Boldt story you used to tell me and Steve, the one about the time Ernie misplaced his mitt and accused a kid of stealing it? Later Ernie found the mitt, and when the kid wanted Ernie to apologize, he refused and said the kid was a thief anyway. The kid go so angry he beat Ernie up; Ernie retaliated by getting the kid kicked off the team for hitting him. Then the coach found out what really happened, and he put the kid back on the team and booted Ernie.

"You used to tell us that story when we fought, each blaming the other for starting it, and you'd dig and dig until you found out how it really got going. Well, something started all the trouble here, and whatever it was, I can't believe it's worth Mom's life. I think you'd better start digging as hard as you used to with me and Steve. You owe it to Mom. To all of us."

Zack went upstairs, and I threw some logs in the fireplace and settled into my chair. As I watched fresh tendrils of flame curling around the logs, I remembered how Ginger shook with anger after Hoot's visit, demanding to know why I quit baseball, as if it were a simple decision from which she was excluded and for which she shouldered the blame. There was truth in her accusation, but it wasn't easy to get to, no easier than it was for those new stalks of flame to get a sufficient grip on the logs to consume them.

I was full of myself when I traveled to Raleigh that first season, positive my stint in the minors would be a brief one. I had solid stats in college and I'd been given a twenty-five-thousand dollar bonus to sign, a hefty sum in those days. It wasn't long, however, before I saw the struggle that lay ahead of me. Even if I did play my best in every game, I would still be bound by the law of averages like everyone else and would get hits only three out of every ten times at bat. In college I played third base, where I had plenty of opportunities to shine; on the Caps I was put in the outfield, where opportunities are fewer and the risk of error is higher. Still, it never occurred to me to do anything other than plug away. All my life I *knew* I was going to be a ball player, so I played my heart out. It wasn't until mid-season when I tore the ligaments in my knee that I thought about what I had seen and heard during those first months. Being in the hospital got me down, even with cute nurses to tease, and my thoughts went in the same direction. I remembered the clubhouse man saying, "What for?" when an older player asked for new bats; the real message was that the guy was on his way out, and he got his marching orders the next day. I remembered the older players who stayed out late at night, knowing that eventually they would be booted out, not up. I remembered overhearing a broken-down catcher say, "I would have done anything–even sold my soul– to play on the majors." And I remembered hearing, over and over again, guys saying things like: *He never got lucky. Some guys don't get lucky. I'd rather have luck than talent.*

If I hadn't been injured, I would have played out the season and returned to Clinton Falls without giving any of that stuff a second thought. Instead, I packed it away and took it back with me the following season.

Ginger's father had never been happy with the idea that his only child was going to marry a baseball player; like my father, he thought in terms of law and medicine. He wanted Ginger to have a safe, comfortable life with a safe, comfortable husband, and baseball didn't fit into that cozy picture. This bothered him, and when something bothered him, he didn't keep it to himself. He asked me what I planned to do if I didn't make it to the majors so often that I did everything short of hiding behind doors to avoid him. The last thing he said to me before I left for Raleigh to start my second season was, "You have a wife now, so this year counts."

As if it didn't count the year before! One isn't

supposed to speak ill of the dead, but he sure could be irritating.

I didn't need Ginger's father to tell me that with a new wife I had new responsibilities. No one ever put more pressure on me than I put on myself. Still, I arrived in Raleigh optimistic, glad to see the fellows and eager to start the season. I was playing well, batting over .300, when Ginger joined me. Scouts hadn't been around much, but after Ginger arrived they started to appear. Within a period of a week or two several guys were called up. Each time someone else was picked, not only could I see Ginger's disappointment, but I could feel mine sinking deep into my gut, heavy as stone. As always, the fellows' talk was about luck: some guys were lucky and some guys weren't. All the stuff I'd thought about in the hospital came creeping back, and I began to wonder in earnest if I was lucky. Really lucky. I knew I was good enough, but so was Sal Capizzi, so was Hoot, so were some of the others. We could all play ball, but only a handful of us would make it to the majors. Luck. Unless a guy was a DiMaggio, a Mantle, a Williams, luck was a deciding factor. I started to notice older guys on opposing teams, men playing out what days they had left with no hope in their eyes. I felt sorry for them and hated myself for it because I would never want to be in a position where younger men would feel sorry for me.

I began to search my life for clues that would tell me if I had luck. I thought about my mother dying, and then my sister, a double tragedy that couldn't be blamed on anything as simple as bad luck. Or could it? Wasn't fate another name for luck? The only real luck I'd had was meeting and marrying Ginger; she was in Raleigh because of me, and her radiance was fading like the dimming of a light. Was I turning good luck into bad?

I don't know when I began to toy with the idea of quitting. At first I resisted the thought. I was raised never to quit anything. Only a man who couldn't measure up quit. Only a coward quit. Only a failure quit. I had always believed in myself, in my ability. I was not a quitter. But I was having trouble with that unknown commodity called luck, and then one night I saw a guy whose name I'd forgotten until Hoot's visit: Methusela.

Although I had forgotten what they called him, I remembered the guy's face, which was creased with deep, sorrowful lines; he looked older than my father. He was put in in the last inning, and he stood hunched over the plate watching the pitcher with a kind of tense desperation that I'd seen in older players: a hit would give them a few more games, maybe a few more weeks, maybe another season. So much hinging on each time up to bat.

Methusela didn't get a hit. He was 3-2 when he swung at a fast-breaking curve ball and missed. I saw the sad slope of his shoulders and dejected tilt of his head as he walked away, and in those few seconds I knew what his life was like, how he felt growing old on the bench, and I knew it was something I could never do. I had too much pride.

I played well that night, hit a double and a homer, but I got on the bus to go back to Raleigh knowing that it would be my last season. I could not trust luck. I could not grow old on the bench. My pride wouldn't allow it.

Hoot noticed my long face and asked if something was bothering me. At first I hesitated, but then I told him my decision. I had the odds all figured out, and they weren't in my favor, or his. I talked about luck and odds and Methusela, about everything with the exception of my bottom-line reason: my pride. I couldn't speak of that to anyone, not even Ginger.

After the bus pulled in, Hoot and I went to a bar and got sloshed. I must have smelled like I had bathed in beer because Ginger turned off the bedroom light as soon as she got a whiff of me. Blind drunk, I stumbled on something and landed on the floor, cursing. I cursed her and the darkness and probably a lot of other things I can't remember anymore. She was crying when I fell asleep.

When I woke in the morning, Ginger was gone. After I showered and dressed and had breakfast, I came back to the room and found her packing. We'd been having a rough time, but seeing her full suitcase was still a shock. Any doubts I'd had about my decision to quit were settled then: I could live without baseball but not without Ginger. I asked her to stay and told her that I was quitting, that this would be the last season. She didn't want me to quit and thought I'd feel differently if she left, but I insisted that she stay so we could leave together. Her eyes were full of questions that I couldn't answer, not then, not ever, and I told her that, too. So we never talked about it, and somehow people came to assume that I'd quit because of her, because she'd hated Raleigh, and I suppose she assumed it herself. I didn't think there was any harm in it. I guess I was wrong. And that's what I'd have to tell her in the morning.

Ginger

I don't remember much about my stay at the cottage. Looking back, it's a feverish blur, days and nights so indistinct that I lost track of time. What I remember most is feeling terribly chilled, so cold that the blood in my veins felt icy, and the coughing. Constant coughing. Coughing and bringing up rust-colored sputum until I had no peace, until all I did was shake and cough. When Zack came for me, I was too exhausted to speak. At the risk of sounding melodramatic, I think I was waiting to die.

The storm was at its height when I turned into what I guessed was the driveway to the cottage. Gale-like winds coming in off the lake were whipping the snow in all directions. My car got stuck in a drift soon after I turned. Instead of staying in the warm car until the storm let up, I took my suitcase and foolishly started out through the blinding snow, moving by instinct. All I could make out of the cottage when I came upon it were the green shutters; the white clapboards were swallowed by snow.

The front door to the cottage opens directly into a large main room that is furnished with comfortable wicker furniture. There is a rough gray stone fireplace in the center of the longest wall, which I knew would be my only source of heat. I put my suitcase down and made trips back and forth to the woodpile behind the cottage. I must have carried nearly a quarter of a cord of firewood, taking as much as I could each trip, to pile on the wide back porch. When I was finished, I was overheated from the effort, but during the time it took to get a strong fire going, I became thoroughly chilled. I thought that being overheated and then chilled is what initially made me ill, but the doctor said my sore throat and headache were early symptoms of my illness.

Luckily, there was an unopened gallon of bottled water in one of the cupboards, as well as a few cans of baked beans that were probably left over from a late summer barbecue. We'd always kept bottled water on hand as an emergency precaution but never any food. Part of Mr. Fowler's job as caretaker is to make sure that there is no food in the kitchen before the cottage is closed for the season. I was grateful he wasn't as thorough as he's always telling us he is.

I moved one of the wicker sofas up to the fireplace and huddled there under worn summer quilts. That's where Zack found me days later. Most of Saturday I cried, desolated by Buddy's rejection. What I had done was wrong and no one knew it better than I, but for him to be unable to stand the sight of me was devastating. I kept remembering the expression on his face, the hard set of his mouth, the way he averted his eyes. And again and again I thought of his father, how all these years he'd kept his vow never to have anything to do with him. But he had never had a relationship with his father. I was his wife. Twenty-seven years of marriage—over thirty years of loving each other—and Buddy wouldn't forgive me. How could he be so hard, I wondered. I'd always been aware that he could be stubborn, at times impossibly unbending; Steve and Zack would complain that his mind was set in concrete when their arguments failed to move him. But his stubbornness was an incidental thing, an occasional swerve off his usual easygoing path. Then I recalled an incident that happened almost twenty years ago. Steve had had a vivid nightmare that he described to me while I was making breakfast. Wide-eyed at the horror of his dream, he told me about slimy green monsters that had huge purple tongues. When Buddy came into the kitchen, Steve rushed up to him and asked him what color his dreams were. "Dreams aren't in color," Buddy said. "They're black and white."

Buddy thinks like he dreams: everything is either black or white. In his world there is no shading, there are no stretched truths or polite lies; it is a place without shadows, without forgiveness.

Heartbroken, I finally understood.

Mr. Fowler came around early Sunday morning, which is the last day I remember clearly. I was putting logs on the fire when I heard the roar of his snowmobile. The intrusive sound and the tracks the vehicle made spoiled the perfect winter scene, but I was relieved he had come. My throat was still sore, and I knew I had a fever.

I tightened the belt to my robe, opened the door and waved. Mr. Fowler carries a gun that he isn't afraid to use, as he is fond of telling the people whose cottages he watches. His eyesight, never good, has deteriorated from cataracts, and in the past few years he has developed a definite palsy in his hands. None of the cottage owners have been able to persuade Mr. Fowler to leave his gun at home when he comes to check on their properties, even though there have been no robberies in years. "It's there in the Constitution," he tells them. "A man has a right to bear arms. A gun is the best protection."

He could kill someone, I thought, watching him get off his snowmobile. When I saw him take his glove off and slip his hand into his pocket to grab hold of his gun, I hoped the someone wouldn't be me. "Mr. Fowler, it's Ginger," I rasped as he trudged toward me, straining to see who I was. With his red wool hat and jacket and his head thrust forward, he looked like Mr. Magoo. I silently cursed the NRA and their lobbying efforts that keep guns in the hands of dim-sighted, trembling old men.

"Ginger?" he said, still unsure as he made his way up the snow-covered steps to the front porch. He was squinting so hard his eyes were slits. I wondered how he managed to drive his snowmobile without crashing into trees.

"Yes, it's Ginger. Please come in."

Thankfully, he took his hand off the gun. "What are you doing here this time of year?" he said, stomping the snow off his boots before stepping inside.

"I was out early yesterday morning when I got caught in the storm," I said, each word scratching my raw throat. "I was too far from home to drive back."

Mr. Fowler pursed his lips, letting me know that

my explanation was insufficient. "I see you got a good fire going, but it ain't enough to heat up this big room. I see you got a suitcase, too."

"I'm going to stay a while. Could you call tomorrow and have the water and the electricity turned on?"

"What about the phone? Do you want the phone or do you have one of them cell phones? You know, your parents used to come out here in the winter, but just for the day. Your mother..."

My mother. I stopped listening, trying to remember when I had last spoken to her. It was the evening before I left for Niagara Falls. She must be worried, I thought, sure that she had called the house. Either Buddy told her I'd left, which I doubted, or he had the answering machine on. My cell phone was dead, and I had forgotten to take the battery charger. If Mr. Fowler had the cottage phone connected, I'd have to tell her why I was there, and I couldn't. But I couldn't let her worry.

Mr. Fowler was still talking; he was reciting a list of the neighbors who had come out to the lake during the winter at one time or another. I'd forgotten how gabby he is. I let him ramble on and tried to look attentive while I thought of a way to let my mother know I was all right. "Mr. Fowler," I said finally, interrupting him, "I don't want the phone connected. It's so peaceful here; nothing should spoil this wonderful quiet. But I would appreciate a favor: could you call my mother and tell her that I'm here and I'm fine?"

"Won't your husband be talking to her?" he said, squinting at me with new interest.

"He's out of town," I said, resenting that I'd been forced to lie.

"How long should I tell her you'll be staying?"

I shrugged. "I don't know."

His eyebrows rose with irritation. "I have to tell her more than what you've given me. She'll have questions."

You have questions, I thought. "Is Jayson's store open?" I said, changing the subject.

"It should be, but you can't get there with your car stuck in that drift like it is."

Then, as sweetly as I could, I asked him to bring me a few things. All I really wanted was orange juice and aspirin, but I gave him a short, sensible list and thirty-five dollars, which would more than cover it. "Thanks for rescuing me," I said, walking him to the door.

"My pleasure," he replied with such old-fashioned gallantry that I had to smile.

Mr. Fowler came back with the groceries and stopped by again on Monday to make sure the utilities were turned on. I opened the door only a crack, thanked him again and told him everything was fine, and shut the door before he could guess that it wasn't. Never in my life had I felt so awful. My fever was worse, and it took all my energy just to breathe. I should have asked for help then, but at the time I didn't know what to do. I couldn't go home, and there was no where else I wanted to go. So I went back to the sofa and crawled under the quilts. Too sick to bother with the fire, I relied on a small electric heater that didn't throw off enough heat to warm a closet. And I got worse. I don't know which day the shaking and chills started or when my breathing got raspy and the coughing became relentless. The only blessing of the illness was that the sicker I became, the less I dwelled upon Buddy and what had happened. By the time Zack and Avery found me, all I wanted was to stop coughing. All I wanted was peace.

The medical attendants on the helicopter must have given me medication in the needles they put in me because I don't remember the flight to the hospital or being taken to a room. I do remember Zack and my mother coming to see me, both looking worried and upset. And then Buddy came. He had two black eyes and a splint on his nose. I recalled Avery's bandaged face and made the connection, but I didn't think about it. Buddy was holding my hand and he was talking about baseball, and I was trying hard to concentrate on what he was saying: "I hated to quit, but I couldn't risk not making it. Hoot was right when he told you I didn't want to grow old on the bench. I never intended for it to hurt you; the decision hurt me enough for both of us. I guess I just couldn't deal with it, and somehow you got the blame. I'm sorry, sweetheart."

He gently squeezed my hand and I closed my eyes, trying to hold back tears. Sick as I was, I knew what his apology had cost him. And I knew what his decision years ago had cost our marriage. A tremendous weariness came over me then, and I drifted off.

Steve brought me back. At first, I had trouble hearing him; it was as if I were dreaming that he was there. But he was real, and I saw how concerned he was. "You're going to get better," he kept saying. "You have to keep fighting. You're going to get well."

And they kept coming back to my room—Steve, Buddy, Zack, and my mother—to give me the same message: *You're going to get better. You're going to get well.* As I explained to the doctor when he commented on my remarkable improvement, I had to get better to get them off my case. Later my mother told me that they had acted deliberately. "It was Steve's idea. He organized us like cheerleaders, insisting that we carry the same message," she said. "I thought he knew what to say because of what had happened to his wrist, but that wasn't it at all. 'Mom can't stand to be told the same thing over and over again,' he said. 'She'll get better just to shut us up.'"

Buddy took me to my mother's house when I was released from the hospital. It was her idea for me to stay there. I was weak and tired easily, in no shape to do much more than recuperate. When we drove up the street where I was raised, where the homes are set far back and large maples shade the sidewalks in the summer, a feeling that I thought was nostalgia came over me. The feeling grew stronger when we drove up to the familiar rambling white house with its crisp black shutters and scarlet front door. I wondered if the odd stab of sentimentality, so strong it brought tears to my eyes, was related to my having been ill, but that wasn't it at all. The feeling disappeared when I stepped inside and didn't come back until Buddy left. Then it returned, stronger than ever, and I knew it wasn't nostalgia: it was relief because I would be living away from Buddy.

My mother insisted upon serving something to friends who came to visit. Buddy arrived for dinner at night, which was additional work. My mother is an excellent cook and Buddy is an appreciative eater, so she has always enjoyed fussing for him. At seventy-five she's aging well, but she's frailer than she used to be, and I could see that the unaccustomed work was too much for her. Each evening she sat in her chair nodding with exhaustion. On the third night I took Buddy aside before we ate and told him that I thought it would better if he didn't have dinner with us for a while. "It's too much for my mother," I said. "She's doing a lot of extra fussing because you're eating with us."

"Well, she shouldn't, and I'll tell her," Buddy said, starting for the kitchen.

I reached out and put my hand on his arm. "She'll insist that it's no bother. Please tell her that you have meetings or something for the rest of the week."

"I can bring dinner—Chinese, Italian—whatever you want."

"She might take your offer the wrong way."

Buddy looked at me for a long moment. I could see questions in his eyes, and hurt. But he didn't say a word before he went into the kitchen to tell my mother that he wouldn't be eating dinner with us for the remainder of the week.

My mother served stuffed breast of veal that night. It was delicious, tender and perfectly seasoned, but I had to force myself to eat. There was a lump in my throat that had nothing to do with my having been ill. I had been quieter than usual during our dinners, but now Buddy was, too. My mother noticed and commented about it. "This is serious food, Thelma," he said. "It deserves all of our attention."

She beamed. "I'm so glad you're enjoying it."

I looked across the table to give him a silent thank you for so graciously handling the situation, but his eyes were focused on the meat he was cutting and when he looked up I saw such sadness that I had to turn away.

The following morning while we were lingering over our breakfast coffee, my mother sat up straighter, as though she needed perfect posture for what she was about to say. "I didn't broach this before, but now that you're looking better I feel that I can. I want you to know why I didn't go to the cottage after Mr. Fowler called to tell me you were there. He mentioned pointedly that you didn't want the phone connected. 'Just the water and the electricity,' he said.

"When I thought about it afterward, I believed that you were giving me a message: you specifically asked him to call me and you didn't want the phone connected. What you were saying—at least what I thought you were saying—was that you wanted to be left alone."

"You're right," I said.

"As the days passed, I found myself in a terrible quandary. I didn't want to call Buddy because I had already left messages on your answering machine, and he didn't call me back. Several times I put my coat on thinking that I'd drive to the cottage to see that you were all right, but I didn't want to intrude. By the time Zack came home I was beside myself with worry."

She paused and leaned forward, holding on to the table. "Ginger, if Zack hadn't come you might have died." Her chin trembled. "What you did was foolish! It was..." She shook her head, unable to say it.

"Stupid," I supplied.

"Yes!" she said, her color rising. "I didn't want to intrude before, and I don't want to now, but I haven't been able to avoid seeing Buddy's broken nose and the bandages on Avery Laird's face. I should mention that I politely suggested to Mr. Laird that there was no point in his waiting at the hospital since he is not a member of the immediate family and wouldn't be allowed to see you. Of course, I thanked him for his concern," she added to assure me that she hadn't been impolite.

Until then I had been afraid to ask. "How did he find me?"

"He hired a detective. Didn't you know?"

I shook my head. "What was his reaction when you suggested that he leave?"

"He went quietly, which is exactly what he should have done. He didn't belong, especially not with Zack there and Buddy nowhere in sight."

Zack. I had been avoiding thinking about Zack and Steve and what they must be thinking. They had undoubtedly talked about the situation and had come to what was an obvious conclusion. I felt embarrassed and ashamed, and at the same time angry. It shouldn't have happened, none of it should have happened.

My mother looked at me expectantly. I had nothing to say.

Early the following afternoon the doorbell rang as I was starting upstairs for a nap. I looked through the peephole (my mother was out playing bridge) and saw Avery. For a second I was tempted not to answer, but hiding wouldn't solve anything. Eventually I'd have to talk to him.

"I apologize for not calling first," he said, handing me a long white florist's box. "Can I stay for a few minutes?"

"Sure," I said, finding it impossible not to stare at the results of Buddy's fury. With the bandages off, Avery's face was a patchwork of stitches and bruises.

I opened the box on the foyer table; inside there were a dozen long-stemmed crimson roses. After I thanked him and hung up his coat, I led him into the living room, then excused myself to put the flowers in water. The roses were gorgeous. As I arranged them in a crystal vase I had taken from the china cabinet, I became conscious that I had no make-up on and that the bathrobe I was wearing had seen better days. Ordinarily this would have bothered me, but now it was unimportant.

Avery was looking out the bay window when I returned. I put the roses on the coffee table, where they looked striking in front of the blue damask sofa. "Windsor is one of the nicest streets in Clinton Falls," he said. "Years ago when I was planning my first upscale subdivision, I must have driven here a half-dozen times. I wanted to create the same feeling of graciousness and permanence, but the subdivision looked raw when it was finished: I hadn't factored age into the equation. That's when I began to appreciate the value of time."

"Windsor has aged well."

"Did you grow up in this house?"

"Yes," I said. "It's much too large for my mother, but she hasn't mentioned moving so I've left the subject alone. Every year she gets a few calls from private buyers asking if she wants to sell. She'll have no trouble when she's ready."

"Buddy is a Clinton Falls native. What street did he live on?"

"Buckingham."

Avery's left eyebrow, which was bisected by a row of diagonal stitches, rose slightly. Buckingham is still the best street in Clinton Falls, a broad avenue lined with huge brick and stone homes. "My childhood was a world away from yours," he said. "When I was seven years old my father left one morning and never came back. He had business problems that led to drinking problems. He couldn't cope and ran away."

"It was rough, but it taught me the most valuable lessons of my life. In the end, I believe I benefited from it."

"How?"

"Because of what my father did, I vowed never to be a quitter. I've always fought as long and as hard as necessary to get what I wanted. And from my mother," he said, his voice noticeably lower, "I learned the most difficult lesson. After my father left, my mother changed almost overnight from a tall, attractive woman who had carried her height gracefully into an entirely different person, stoop-shouldered and defeated looking. It was as if she had become someone else. The look was still there when she died at the age of seventy."

He paused reflectively. The winter sun coming in through the large windows shone mercilessly on the yellowing bruises on his face. "I learned by my mother's example that if you think of yourself as a victim, you'll be one," he said. His eyes, an intense green, met mine. "All my life I've pushed forward no matter what happened. I've never allowed anything to defeat me."

Suddenly I felt weak and slightly dizzy. "I think I'd better sit for a moment."

Avery's arm was around me instantly. He led me to the sofa where he carefully placed me on a cushion as though I were breakable. "Can I get you anything?" he said with concern.

"I was just a little lightheaded. It'll pass."

"I've been so worried about you," he said, sitting beside me. "The day your son and I found you at the cottage I was afraid we were too late. And then being banished from the hospital—I can't blame your mother, but that was hard."

He placed his hand on mine. "I don't want to push because you've been so ill, but you have to know that nothing has changed for me except that I'm even more in love with you than I was before. When you didn't come in to work after we went to Niagara Falls and I couldn't reach you, I was nearly wild with worry. It was so out of character for you not to show up and not to call. And when I went to your house and Buddy didn't know where you were, I was ready to turn the world upside down to find you."

"You went to my house?"

"You didn't know?"

I shook my head, aware from his surprise that I had told him more than I should have. Buddy and I had carefully avoided any mention of Avery; we had carefully avoided saying much about anything.

"How long will you be staying here?"

"I'm not sure."

"Marry me, Ginger."

"Please," I said, withdrawing my hand.

"I'm sorry. I promised I wouldn't push. We'll take it one step at a time. When do you think you'll be well enough to come back to work?"

"I... I won't be coming back."

"Why not?" he demanded.

"It should be obvious."

"A number of things have become obvious," he said, "and the fact that we belong together is one of them. I'll hold off working on plans for the first phase of the Leverton development until you're ready."

"No, Avery."

"I'll wait," he said determinedly. "I want you more than I have ever wanted anything, and I'm going to win you!"

"I'm not a prize!" I said. "And I'm not in love with you."

"Maybe not yet," he said with a smile, "but you will be."

I shook my head. "You're indomitable. Don't you ever accept a refusal?"

"Just being with you makes me happy. I never thought I'd feel this way." His expression became serious. "Years ago something happened that has haunted me," he said. "When I first started out in real estate, I won a bid on a large parcel of land by several hundred dollars. The man whose bid was closest to mine, a successful developer who'd been around for a long time, came up to me one day soon afterward. 'You did your homework on that one,' he said, 'but it was luck that pulled you through. A fellow can have luck like yours a few times or he can have a lifetime of it, but I've never seen it fail that he has to pay one way or another.' I interpreted what he said as the bitter words of a sore loser and forgot about it until six months later, when my son came down with encephalitis that damaged two-thirds of his brain.

"I don't consider myself superstitious, but there were times when I thought of that developer and wondered if what he said to me was a curse. I always wanted a family, yet year after year I ate holiday dinners at other men's tables. I was tired of dating, tired of fielding divorcees anxious to grab another meal ticket, tired of younger women with whom I have nothing in common. I had so much to share and found myself more and more alone. Then I met you."

"But I'm married," I said. "How could you even think...?"

"I didn't think. I fell in love."

"Is that why you offered me the job?" I looked at him hard. "The truth."

His face was open. "Sure, I wanted you with me. I couldn't see enough of you. But even before we finished our first lunch together at Treehaven I saw that you had creativity, great instincts, and sound judgment—an unbeatable combination. You proved it with the Leverton deal: you saved me over half a million dollars."

"Six hundred fifty thousand for starters," I said. "The Leverton property is easily worth well over five million. You were willing to go to six million if you had to."

He smiled. "I won't argue."

"You used me when you took me to that meeting with Ernie Boldt."

"I wouldn't put it quite that way, although I did handle it badly. Your wariness afterward let me know it, which made me afraid I might have hurt my chances with you."

I threw my hands up in exasperation. "How can you sit there and calmly talk about your chances with me?"

He leaned toward me, so close I knew he wasn't wearing aftershave lotion. "I'm fifty-two years old. I've made a lot of mistakes that I've had to live with. If I've learned nothing else, I know that chances for real happiness are rare, and when I met you, I knew you were my chance," he said, as though courting me was the only logical thing he could have done under the circumstances.

"And my being married didn't concern you?"

"I figured that if you were truly happy with your husband, you couldn't be lured away. But if you weren't..."

Unable to listen anymore, I stood up. "I think you'd better leave."

Avery rose reluctantly. Despite the battering his face had taken, he looked anything but beaten. There was determination in the set of his chin and desire in his eyes. "I have something to say first: if your marriage was all that it should be, you wouldn't have gone to the cottage; nor would you be staying here with your mother. You were unhappy weeks before we went to Niagara Falls, and as for what happened there—our being together—nothing that good could have been good for only one of us."

He cupped my face in his hands. "I feel bad for all that you've been through, especially your illness.

You've had a rough time, but it's almost over. We have the rest of our lives..."

I removed his hands, interrupting him. "You're like an inflatable stand-up toy my sons had when they were little: it was a clown that popped back up every time they punched it down."

"I've been called worse," he said with a slight smile. "And I'll keep coming back, like that clown, until you marry me."

My head reeled.

I didn't walk him to the door. He let himself out.

The first thing my mother noticed when she came home was the roses. "Oh, how lovely," she said, bending so she could better admire them. "When was Buddy here?"

"Buddy didn't bring them. Avery Laird stopped by this afternoon."

She straightened instantly, as though the flowers had turned suddenly foul-smelling. "Really," she said.

During dinner I felt her disapproving silence like a rebuke. I didn't know what to say. I didn't know what I wanted, and exhausted from Avery's visit, I was in no shape to make any decisions. Since I had gotten out of the hospital I had struggled over what to do next. It was difficult enough to forgive Buddy for all the years he let me carry the blame for his quitting baseball. But to then have to forgive him for wanting me to leave because he couldn't stand the sight of me, no matter how much he was hurting, and to forgive him yet again for making no attempt to look for me after I had been gone for days, and yet again for letting Zack and my mother cope alone when I was taken to the hospital, was almost more than I could do.

While I was at the cottage, getting sicker by the hour, I kept hoping he could come for me, and when he didn't, a kernel of disappointment grew inside me that was more uncomfortable than the fever and the chills and the incessant coughing, disappointment that grew heavy as a stone and stayed after the other symptoms disappeared. Every time I saw Buddy or thought of him I felt that heaviness, like a weight of despair, and knew that nothing—not our marriage, not our relationship—would ever be the same again.

While we were having our coffee, my mother cleared her throat. "Tell me," she said, "how are you going to explain the roses if Buddy stops by tonight?"

She waited for my reply, the expression on her face troubled. "I hadn't thought about that," I said.

"Just what are you thinking?" she said, peering at me as though searching for clues that would explain my behavior.

I sighed, again feeling the stone of disappointment that always seemed to be with me. "I've been trying not to think."

"Well," she said, "I have been thinking. I may be old, but I can still add, especially when all the numbers are so clear: you went to Niagara Falls with Avery Laird; after you came back you went to the cottage; Mr. Laird hired a detective to find you, and his feelings for you are very apparent, at least to me.

"You're an adult, but I'm still your mother, and whether you want it or not, I'm going to give you some advice. You and Buddy have had a long, happy marriage—twenty-seven years—which is more than half your life. To jeopardize the most important relationship you've ever had is foolish, just plain foolish!"

I stared at her, shocked. "You think I'm deliberately having an affair with Avery?"

Despite her professed modernity, my mother is a bit Victorian. Pink spots of embarrassment dotted her cheeks. "The... That's what it looks like."

"And you think we had sex here this afternoon?" I said, unable to suppress a smile.

"Please, Ginger, is that really necessary?"

"Yes," I said, "because what you're thinking didn't happen. I told Avery I wouldn't be going back to work for him. He wants to marry me; he's been courting me for a while. I refused him again today."

"Courting you?" she said, astonished. "How can he court you? You're already married!"

"Avery Laird is accustomed to going after what he wants."

"What about the Commandment: *Thou shall not covet another man's wife*? Or is it *thy neighbor's wife*?" She shook her head. "I suppose it really doesn't matter. Whatever happened to simple decency? It seems that no one respects anything anymore."

"Nothing might have happened if Buddy and I hadn't been having problems." I hesitated. "I want to ask you something, and I'd like you to take your time answering. You and Dad must have discussed it when Buddy quit baseball. What conclusions did you come to?"

She didn't attempt to hide her surprise. "You've never wanted to talk about it."

"I do now," I assured her.

"Dad thought Buddy quit because you were so unhappy in Raleigh, and it worried him. He hated the idea of your being married to a baseball player, but he hated even more the thought that Buddy was stopped from realizing his potential because of your unhappiness: 'Your inability to adjust,' he said.

"Your father believed that the husband's career always came first. He was old-fashioned, in some respects a chauvinist," she said, quickly adding, "may he rest in peace."

Even my father blamed me. "And what did you think?"

"Honestly, I didn't know. I was aware of how much you hated Raleigh, but I couldn't believe, like your father did, that you held Buddy back. Maybe I'm flattering myself, but I've always felt that I understood you—until these past few weeks, anyway—and I couldn't imagine your doing something as selfish as standing in Buddy's way. You've always been a giver, not a taker."

"I didn't stand in his way. Buddy made the decision on his own. He was afraid he might not make it to the majors, and he didn't want to grow old on the bench."

My mother nodded. "I can understand that."

"So can I," I said, tears starting down my cheeks, "and I could have understood then if he'd told me. But he didn't. He never discussed it with me, not once, and all these years I've felt guilty."

"Maybe he didn't realize..."

"He couldn't deal with it so he let me take the blame, which I did and I felt terrible, as though I were solely responsible."

The doorbell rang, startling us. The door was locked, and Buddy didn't have a key. My mother recovered first. "I'll put the roses in the garage and get the door while you splash cold water on your face," she said with crisp efficiency.

My eyelids were slightly puffy, but Buddy didn't notice. He helped clear the table, and then my mother shooed us out of the kitchen. "I can think better when I'm working by myself," she said.

"You must be anticipating some pretty important thoughts," Buddy teased.

"I hope I get one or two," she said.

After we went into the living room, Buddy put his arms around me. He was wearing jeans and a thick gray wool sweater that felt rough against my face. "I miss you," he said, nibbling at my neck. His hands slid down my back and he pressed me to him. If things had been right between us, my body would have responded as it always did, melting into his like a wave curling into the shore. Instead, my spine was stiff, unforgiving. I felt his arms drop. "I'm sorry," I said. "I guess it'll take time."

He thrust his hands into his pockets and bent his head. When he looked up, his eyes searched my face. "I've been cleaning the house—dishes done, rugs vacuumed. It looks pretty good. When can I take you home?"

Home. I didn't want to think about it. "I still tire easily."

"You wouldn't have to do anything."

"I know."

An awkward silence followed that Buddy finally broke. "How about a date, then? Will you be up to going out to dinner with me Friday night?"

"Sure," I said, forcing a smile before turning

away in the hope that he wouldn't see how my heart ached for him, how it ached for us because I knew in that instant that I wouldn't be going home. Our marriage was over.

After Buddy left I started to tremble. Alone. I was going to be alone. The thought terrified me. All night I tossed, worrying about where I would live, how I would support myself. I tossed and I cried. I wept for me and for Buddy, for Steve and for Zack and for my mother, for all that we'd had and were about to lose.

Toward dawn I started thinking about Jane, who went back to Florida after she flew to Clinton Falls to see me in the hospital when I was moved out of intensive care. I'd told her it wasn't necessary for her to visit but she came anyway, insisting that she had to see for herself that I was going to be all right. Despite her tan, she looked anxious and unsettled, as though she'd sat in the sun out of duty and not for pleasure. I asked her how things were going. "Nothing's happening," she said, her shoulders sagging. "My life feels empty, like it's lost its purpose. As horrible as it was, even the divorce gave me something to focus on. Now I have nothing. I've been trying to figure out how to start again, but it isn't easy. All I can think of is buying out Cal's interest in the stores and running them myself. I'll probably do it; I just wish I could come up with more choices."

I wondered if I would start looking as anxious as Jane, who until her divorce had always appeared relaxed and self-confident. The long night I had spent certainly revealed my lack of choices. Since working for Avery was out of the question, my only option would be to go back to selling real estate while I tried to use whatever remaining time I had to develop a career as a writer. The future looked as bleak as the light in my room.

My mother was up early. I heard the stairs creak and decided to get out of bed. Since I had been staying with her I had become sensitive to her routine, to the pace of her days. Mornings, which had been her best time when she was younger, were now the most difficult part of the day for her. She woke stiff with arthritis, and it took a while before she could get moving with relative ease. She had also become preoccupied with sleep. The first thing she said to me each morning was, "How did you sleep?" as though the prognosis for the day, positive or negative, depended upon my answer. Apparently she was having difficulty sleeping—age, she explained--so it pleased her if I slept well.

It was the first morning that she didn't ask how I'd slept. She took one look at me when I walked into the kitchen and asked if I'd like juice or coffee first. My throat felt dry. "Juice," I said. "I'll get it."

I poured the juice and put a slice of bread in the toaster. I wasn't hungry but knew that I had to eat something, because it would upset her if I didn't. "What would you like for dinner tonight?" she asked.

The last thing I wanted was to think about dinner, but again, I knew my mother; if I didn't make a suggestion, we'd have to discuss it. "Let's do something with the chicken that was leftover from last night."

"Then we can have fish tomorrow night. Friday is always the best day for fish. It's the freshest."

"I'm going out to dinner with Buddy tomorrow

night."

"You are?" she said. "I'm so glad!"

Her happy relief made me feel like a fraud, as though I were setting her up for disappointment. I had no choice. I had to tell her. "It isn't..." I began. "I'm not..." It was impossible.

She looked at me apprehensively. "What are you trying to say?"

We were sitting opposite each other. I got up and knelt at her side. "Buddy and I will be separating. I made the decision last night. I'm going to tell him tomorrow."

My mother's face crumpled like a child's; her chin trembled and her eyes filled with tears. "No!" she said. "No!"

I put my arm around her, trying not to cry, but when she reached into her bathrobe pocket with a shaking hand to pull out a tissue, I felt her sadness and my composure cracked. "I'm sorry," I said, wiping tears away.

She blew her nose. "Is it because he let people think you were the reason he left baseball?"

"Partly."

"What he did was wrong, but can't you find it in your heart to forgive him? It's hard for me to believe that he intentionally hurt you."

"It's more than just baseball."

She sat quietly, probably wondering what my other reasons were, but to her credit she didn't ask. "You know," she said finally, "there were times when I got awfully mad at your father—he could be infuriating—but eventually my anger would pass. I've always thought of those times as bad spells, hard to live through but not worth destroying what we'd built."

"I can't go back. It's over."

My mother sighed so deeply that her disappointment was audible. "I love Buddy as much as if he were my son."

"That doesn't have to change. A part of me will always love him, too."

"What will you do? How will you manage?"

"I'll have to sell real estate again."

"For that awful Earl Diamond?" she said, shuddering.

"The real estate market is terrible now, so I can't afford to be choosy. I'll also work to establish myself as a writer. I have a solid credential, which is a good first step. I'm going to call Cordell Wylie, the editor of *Forum*, today. I want to do another interview. There are also real estate publications that I can contact. Maybe I'll be a late bloomer," I said, trying to sound positive, "and eventually be able to support myself as a writer. A middle-aged success."

She smiled wanly. "I hate to see this happen."

"So do I."

She rose stiffly, holding on to the table for support. I noticed how enlarged her knuckles were, how the skin on the backs of her hands had become so thin it was nearly transparent. Once her hands had been beautiful; now they were the hands of an old woman. I had always felt the responsibility of being an only child, but never more than I did then. With my father gone there was no one she loved more than me, and at a time in her life when she should be having untroubled days, I was causing her worry and unhappiness. I wished I could tell her that I changed my mind, or that it would only be a temporary separation and eventually Buddy and I would get back together, but I couldn't. I owed her the truth, and as sad and frightened as I was, I knew there was no other way.

Buddy

I should have known what was coming because
the signs were there, from Ginger's quick and grateful
acceptance of Thelma's suggestion that she stay at her
house when she was released from the hospital to
Ginger's request that I stop eating dinners with them.
But even when I felt Ginger's back stiffen under my
hands when I held her, I still tried to excuse it. I
attributed her behavior to her illness and told myself
that time would take care of things. I tried to ignore
what was happening because I didn't want it to
happen. I didn't want her to tell me that our marriage
was over.

We had a date for dinner on Friday night. I had
planned on stopping at Thelma's to see her on
Thursday, but sleet started coming down late in the
afternoon, making driving dangerous, so I called to
tell her that I wouldn't be coming by. "What time do
you want me to pick you up tomorrow night?" I said.

"Whenever you want."

"I'll be there before six so we can beat the Friday
night dinner crowd," I said.

My attitude toward clothes has always been

casual: as long as what I was wearing was clean, didn't have any holes in embarrassing places, and was within range of being appropriate, there was nothing to be concerned about. But to please Ginger, I put on gray flannel slacks, a fresh button-down shirt, and a navy blazer for our dinner date. She was waiting for me when I arrived. Despite having a week of Thelma's great cooking, she was so thin that the red sweater and black slacks she was wearing looked like they had been borrowed from someone who was several sizes larger. She was pale and hollow-eyed, as though she hadn't slept. "Are you sure you're up to going out?" I said, shocked. She looked better when she left the hospital.

"Positive," she said.

The sudden change in her appearance was the strongest signal yet, like a shout warning of an avalanche as stones start tumbling down, but I held her coat as though nothing unusual was happening, as though I couldn't see the sadness in her eyes or feel the nervous thumping of my heart.

We went to an Italian restaurant that was one of our favorites. She ordered a special dish they were offering, ravioli stuffed with seafood, but she didn't do more than pick at it. My appetite wasn't much better. When people we knew stopped at our table to chat, I was grateful because I could put my fork down. Our plates were nearly full when the waiter came to collect them; he asked if there was something wrong with our dinners. "They were fine," I said. "Why don't you pack them up, and we'll take them with us."

The parking lot was icy, so I told her to wait while I got the car. I carried our dinners in a brown paper bag, my eyes stinging as I walked, but it wasn't from the cold. When I got into the car, I swallowed hard and turned the key in the ignition. There was nothing else I could do.

She told me she would like to go home to pick up a few things. Then she paused. "And to talk," she said.

We went into the house through the garage. "Who brought my car back?" she asked.

"The boys," I said.

She stood in the front hall looking around. "Being here feels strange," she said.

I took off my coat, hung it in the closet, and held out my hand for hers. She shook her head. "I'm not staying. Buddy, I want a divorce."

For a minute or so I didn't breathe. I felt that everything had stopped: my heart, my pulse, my life. She was talking, but it was hard to hear what she was saying. My ears felt like they had filled with blood.

"Please, Buddy, say something."

"I don't want a divorce!"

Tears glittered in her eyes. "It's over. It'll never be the same. We can't go back."

"It doesn't have to be the same. Relationships change."

"Can you look at me and tell me that you'll never think of me and Avery Laird when we're together?" she said. "And by *together*, I don't mean only when we're having sex—when we're taking a walk on a nice summer evening or sitting in the family room watching television. Something will remind you, or maybe nothing will remind you. The thought will suddenly surface: it will be there, and it will chase everything else out of your mind."

"Eventually, with time..."

"There will never be enough time," she said, her tears now coming fast. "Just as there will never be enough time for me to forget the blame I've carried all these years for your quitting baseball, or to forgive you for always putting yourself before me."

"I love you."

I stepped toward her with my arms open, but she backed away. She was crying hard, almost hysterically. "Don't you understand? Love isn't enough. What we had was... it was special... but it's gone. I see things differently now. I see you differently."

She ran upstairs, sobbing. I went into the family room and sank into my chair.

I don't know how long I was sitting there before she came into the family room carrying the bag that held our uneaten dinners. "I'll put these in the refrigerator," she said. "I'm taking my car back to my mother's."

She paused. "On Monday I'm going to call Neil Hamilton. I want him to represent me. We shouldn't have any problems working things out; there isn't much in the way of material assets. Let's not make it any harder on each other than it already is."

Then I asked her. I couldn't stop myself. "Are you going back to work for Laird?"

She smiled slightly, acknowledging what I'd done. "No," she said, "and I've already told him."

I wanted to ask her when she talked to him, and where, and what was said. But I held it all in. I didn't utter a word.

And she left.

The first weeks of our separation were as hellish as any I've ever lived through, the worst moments being when we told the boys. Neither Ginger nor I wanted to do it, but they had us in a corner when they kept asking why she wasn't home. Although they probably made some educated guesses about Laird and her stay at the cottage, I still think it came as a surprise to them. We would have liked to at least tell Zack in person, but there was a snowstorm in Ithaca on the weekend we'd asked him to come home, so we told him on the telephone, each on an extension. I don't recall who said what. All I remember is Zack's silence, as long and agonizing as a howl. Steve's reaction was similar, except his came out as an anguished, "Nooooo," that cut through our hearts.

"This is the saddest divorce I've ever seen," I said to Ginger after we finished talking to Steve.

"You're right."

"We could try..."

"No," she said.

Zack came home the second weekend in March to celebrate his first acceptance to a medical school. Ginger was still getting settled in an apartment so he stayed with me, a pattern that will probably continue until we sell the house. We all went out to dinner—Ginger and me, Zack and Thelma—and for a little while it was like it used to be. But then the dinner was over and we went our separate ways, the spell broken. It was painful to have a taste of being a family again and to lose it so quickly.

On the Wednesday of the following week we signed a separation agreement in Neil Hamilton's office, which was as somber as a funeral parlor with its dark wood furniture and maroon leather chairs. Neil looked almost as sad as I did. "You've always seemed so well suited for each other," he said. "Even working out the terms of your agreement was the most amiable I've ever seen. Speaking as a friend, I hate to see this."

"Me, too," I said.

Ginger didn't say anything.

He shook our hands. "If you decide to go through with a divorce, I can file the agreement and the other necessary papers a year from now."

For me, Neil's words were like a shot that signals the beginning of a race: I had a year to get her back.

Word spreads fast in a place the size of Clinton Falls. Women started calling me in earnest after Ginger and I signed the agreement (some had called me before), so many women that it reminded me of when Steve and Zack were in junior high and the girls' hormones were doing somersaults; the telephone rang and rang, driving us nuts. But now that the calls are for me, I don't mind them, at least most of them. I've been invited to dinners and to concerts, to movies and to plays. Women have asked me to play tennis and racquetball with them. One woman got right to the point and asked me to play with her. After I got over the shock of her invitation, we both laughed. She's a woman Ginger and I have known for years, someone who always seemed so prim and proper that I still shake my head when I think about it. "A divorced woman my age can't afford to be shy," she said, "especially not when a man who appeals to her suddenly becomes available." It was harder to refuse her than it was to refuse the others; it's one thing to say no to a meal or a movie and quite another to have to tell a woman that you aren't interested in her. I hope I don't get another invitation like that one.

All the attention would be flattering if I weren't aware that there are considerably more unattached middle-aged women around than there are men for them. Some nights when I'm about to microwave a frozen dinner I think of those nice invitations, but that's as close as I get to accepting one. I want Ginger to know that she is the only woman I care about, and if everyone in Clinton Falls knows it as well, that's even better. In fact, my lack of interest in developing a social life has already gotten to her. She called to tell me that she heard I'd been refusing invitations. "You have to start going out," she said. "You can't stay home like a hermit."

"I'm not a hermit," I said. "I'm out every day. I teach, I play tennis..."

"That's not what I mean. You need a social life, female companionship."

"Will you go out with me?"

"Oh, Buddy!" She tried to sound exasperated, but she started to laugh.

Her laughter was the first sign of encouragement I'd had, and I pounced on it. "Seriously, can't we still be friends? Let me take you out to dinner."

Waiting for her reply was agonizing. "I'm not ready to do that."

We had that conversation at the beginning of April. It is now the end of the month. She called last night to tell me that *Forum* accepted an interview article she just completed and that she has an assignment to start another one; she also placed a short article in a slick real estate magazine. Thinking that the purpose of her call was to share her good news, my hopes soared. "Congratulations," I said. "You're off to a great start. What you need is more time..."

She interrupted before I could continue. "That's why I'm calling. I know I need more time to write. Avery Laird has been after me to work with him on developing the Leverton property. It will be a maximum of thirty hours a week at my former salary. I won't have to run out at night or on weekends like I do now. I've decided to accept his offer and wanted you to know before you heard it from someone else."

Laird. I had all I could do not to shove my fist through the wall. "No," I protested, "I'll give you the money."

"You can't afford it."

What she said was true, but she said it so matter-of-factly that it felt like a kick in the groin. My status, my power, whatever it is that earns respect has always come from my skills, not my pockets. "That hurt," I said.

She apologized, and from the tone of her voice I knew that she meant it. My instincts told me that it was the perfect moment to ask her out to dinner again, so I did and she accepted.

Our date is for tomorrow evening. She'll be skittish, afraid that I'll try to pressure her into rejecting Laird's offer and anxious that I might attempt to seduce her or worse, appeal for sympathy by acting lost and lonely. There is truth in every one of those temptations; she knows me well. But I know her equally well, possibly better because of the hard thinking I've done. I'll show her as early in the evening and as subtly as I can that she can expect exemplary behavior from me. No one knows better than I how to make Ginger relax. And then we'll talk. We have a lot to talk about. In a few weeks we'll be going to the boys' graduations, Steve's at Harvard and Zack's at Cornell. After we discuss our plans, I'll broach the subject of Zack's summer employment, which has been on both our minds. Zack has applied to the DeWitt Clinton Cancer Center here in Clinton Falls for a summer job, and to Roswell Park Cancer Institute in Buffalo, where he'll be going to medical school in the fall. When I spoke to him tonight, he told me that Roswell Park made him a nice offer; he still hasn't heard from the Clinton Center. Zack took our break-up very hard; from what he said, I know he'll lean towards Buffalo no matter what the Clinton Center offers. "I can't stand seeing you and Mom living the way you are now," he said.

Gently, very gently, I'll tell her how he feels. For years she worried that both boys would leave Clinton Falls after they were grown; with Steve it was almost a certainty, so she put her hopes in Zack. There was nothing she wanted more than for Zack to return permanently to Clinton Falls after he was finished with his education. Although he didn't say it, I'm sure Zack knows how she feels. I'll tell her that even if Zack accepts the offer, it's only for this summer. There is always next summer. Things could change.

Zack's wasn't the only call I received tonight. I also heard from Thelma. "Ginger mentioned that she told you about Avery Laird's offer," she said.

"Unfortunately."

"I was up all last night, thinking and thinking. I don't like Avery Laird. He has no sense of decency, none whatsoever. So I decided to make her a better offer. This morning I contacted a couple who called me in February, and I asked them if they were still interested in buying my house. They said they were, and I told them I'd get back to them. Then I called Ginger and made my offer. I told her that I wanted her to negotiate the sale and that all the proceeds would be hers, providing that she doesn't go to work for Avery Laird, so she can concentrate on becoming a writer."

"What was her reaction?"

"She said it was a bribe. I disagreed and told her to consider it the graduate school education that her father and I never gave her. I also made the point that she was going to eventually get the money anyway, and that it would give me pleasure to see her putting it to good use now. I certainly don't need it. I have more than enough."

I have always liked Thelma, but at that moment I was crazy about her. "Did she accept?" I asked eagerly.

"She's thinking about it, which is the reason I'm calling. She mentioned that she's going out to dinner with you tomorrow night. I hope she decides to accept before then, but if she doesn't and she should happen to tell you about it, I don't want her to feel pressured. Ginger doesn't take kindly to being pressured."

"I know," I said. "But Thelma, are you sure you want to do this? You love your house."

"I love my daughter, not my house. I should have sold the house ages ago; it's far too big for me. I stayed for the wrong reasons, clinging to the past. It's time to move on. I'm already beginning to look forward to living in an apartment—no more stairs to climb, no worries about hiring people to mow the grass and plow the driveway."

"You're a remarkable woman."

"That's kind, but it isn't true. I'm just doing what I think is right." She paused. "I've missed you, Buddy."

"Don't count me out yet."

"Oh, I'm not," she assured me. "I'd never do that."

After we hung up, I remembered a baseball story about a huddle between Tony Lazzeri, a Yankee second baseman, and Lefty Gomez, the great Yankee pitcher. During a game when the bases were loaded and no one was out, Lazzeri called for time. He trotted over to the pitcher's box, looked Gomez in the eye, and said, "You got yourself into this; get yourself out."

I recalled the story, but I couldn't remember whether Gomez managed to get himself out of that one. In any case, I know how he felt. Living in this house without Ginger is a constant reminder of what I got myself into. Now I have to get myself out of it, and I will: I'll win her back. Even if she doesn't accept Thelma's offer, which is almost impossible to imagine, I still have hope. Laird may have money, but I know my wife: I know what pleases her, what charms her, what irritates her. As I mentioned earlier, I've had time to do a lot of thinking, particularly about the observations Zack made after Ginger was taken to the hospital. I saw myself through my son's eyes, and it wasn't pleasant.

Tomorrow night Ginger and I will be having dinner together, and in a few weeks we'll go to Ithaca and to Boston, where we'll bask in the light of our sons' successes. We'll celebrate the ties that connect us, and Ginger will begin to soften. Then, after the graduations are over, I'll wait a week or two and invite her out to dinner again. And during the evening when I sense the moment is right, I'll tell her that I've decided not to coach football in the fall.

I have no illusions. Winning her back won't be easy, but I keep telling myself that it can be done. Once in my life I let go of a dream. I quit because even though I had the skill, I didn't trust my luck. Not this time.

NOTE FROM THE AUTHOR

While I was writing The Last Season, The Story of a Marriage, I came to love Buddy and Ginger. They are charming, good people, characters I would want to have as friends. It was tempting to give them a conclusive, happy ending, to wrap up their lives in a neat package, but when the time came to do that, I couldn't. I have too much respect for them. I couldn't give them a pat ending because life doesn't give us pat endings. Instead, it gives us hope, which is what they have at this point in their story.

Questions For Discussion

1. Ginger and her best friend, Jane Thacker, were stay-at-home moms, a luxury many women don't have today. Did they make the right choice in light of the fact that they are in marriages that are ending and they don't have satisfying careers? How do you see their present lives and their prospects for the future?

2. At the beginning of the novel, Buddy and Ginger have a happy marriage. Ideally, marriage should be a fifty-fifty partnership, but in most marriages one partner gives more than the other to make the relationship work. Which partner gives the most in the Middletons' marriage, and what percentage does that partner give?

3. After Ginger tells Buddy that she's never seen Cal Thacker think of anyone but himself, Buddy is quieter than usual. Later, he is amazing in bed. Why doesn't Ginger give more than glancing recognition to the self-centeredness in Buddy that she sees in Cal?

4. Early in the novel, Ginger has lunch with Avery Laird at the Treehaven Country Club. When Avery calls her son's injury a tragedy, Ginger disagrees. How does her interpretation of the meaning of tragedy relate to the novel?

5. Why does Buddy's frequent praise for Ginger's cooking seem patronizing? Is this intentional on his part?

6. In what ways does Buddy's marriage resemble his parents' marriage?

7. Buddy blames Ginger when people ask him why he quit baseball; he tells them that his wife was unhappy, that she would have left him. Why does Buddy refuse to talk to Ginger about why he quit? Why does he insist upon their agreement never to discuss it?

8. How have Buddy's skills as an athlete given him a satisfying life?

9. What role does money play in the novel?

10. What role does luck, or the belief in luck, have in the novel?

11. What is the significance of the title, *The Last Season*?

12. Which man do you believe will win Ginger: Buddy or Avery? Or will neither one win?

Come visit my website for your free story!

www.mariandschwartz.com